GABRIEL'S ROAD

A NOVELLA OF THE DEVIL'S WEST

LAURA ANNE GILMAN

Cover Art: Alma Ortega
Cover Design: Natania Barron
Editor: Leah Cutter
Copy Editor: Sarah Craft
Production: April Steenburgh

Print ISBN 978-1-61138-797-1
eBook ISBN 978-1-61138-796-4

for everyone who has ever thought "there's nothing I can do" and did it anyway.

No story begins at the beginning. Before there was wind there was water, and before water there was bone, and before bone there was magic, but magic does not exist without wind, water and bone.

So too, every story begins before the start.

1

The Banks of the Mudwater, Then

THE LAST CLEAR *memory he had was a voice, worried, male. Not his. "This is madness. You'll die before you make it to the river."*

"If I don't make it, I'll die. You think this is what I want? This is everything I didn't want. It's not giving me a choice." Then hands tossing clothing into a valise, latching it shut with fingers that trembled.

His voice. His hands.

After that, time disappeared, a cracked slate half-wiped clean, the remaining letters indecipherable. There was hazy recollection of retching over the side, knees sore on wood, his stomach heaving painfully, bile in his mouth and fever in his bones. Then the feel of water lapping at his arms and chest, and a bluish haze and blessed nothingness.

Briefly he'd risen enough to grasp at the smell of sick and mud, and then he lost even that, sinking back again into the bluish haze where nothing hurt. Nothing tugged at him, dragging him back against his will.

You'll die.

You'll die.

Awareness returned slowly, the faint curl of light over the mountains. But it remained dark where he was, a thick fog wrapped around him, muting sound and sensation. It bothered him, that lack of sensation, enough that he fought it, as though sheer force of will would push the fog from him.

But nothing changed, and he fell back, finally, exhausted.

You'll die.

Had he died?

Am I dead? The thought, oddly, did not disturb him.

"Nah, stop that." An ancient voice, and he had conflicting thoughts of a wizened willow-stick, twisted and fragile, and a bar of iron, fresh-cooled from the forge.

Elder. And, *Medicine woman.*

"Stop that," the voice said again, and with her voice came other sounds, chanting in a language he did not know, the rise and fall of the words like the flow of tides, no possible end or beginning but a constant circle, turning in on themselves like....like... He knew what it was like but it would not come to him, the idea lingering in that blurred haze just beyond his reach.

"Stop fighting so hard," the ancient voice told him, a gentle scold. "Let it come and let it go."

Let what come, and let it go where? The question tickled at him, then faded. He thought there were hands on him, though he could not have said where his body was, or where it was being touched.

"We've healing yet to do, and it won't be done with you interfering."

He wasn't dead, then?

The hands, real or not, were warm, so warm he had no choice but to follow them, to fall into the cup of them as the tides rolled over and misty shores closed in around him, and all he could hear was chanting, filling his ears and sliding into his bones.

Heal, the voice said, inside the fog, under the waters, inside him, and his body had no choice but obey.

THE FOG SEEMED thinner when he resurfaced. The chanting had paused, or stopped entire, and silence wrapped around him, a curious silence waiting for something to fill it.

He tried to speak, but all that came out was a pained grunt. In the shadows around him there was the sound of cloth moving against cloth, something heavy shifting. Trying to see what it was, he realized his eyes were still closed. Opening them took effort, his lashes gummed together as though he'd slept too long after too much drink.

At first the world was a pale pink blur, then something pressed on his... shoulder, yes, his shoulder, he could feel his body now, piece by piece, and a whisper came, instructing him to close his eyes once again.

Obedient, he did so. Something soft and damp touched his eyelids, wiping slowly until the whisper instructed him to try once again.

This time his lids opened easily, the pink blur resolving into the soft flicker of firelight. He breathed with the knowledge of *firelight* and *eyes* before turning his head—*yes, he had a head, and a neck and chest and limbs, warmly wrapped in furs* — to see who the soft voice belonged to.

A young boy looked back at him, maybe nine but no more than eleven, whose wide black eyes made him think of... something, but he could not recall what, or who.

"You are awake," the boy said, shaping the English words carefully, as though still uncertain of them. "I will fetch grandmother." And then he was gone, moving quickly but quietly. Without him, the space seemed to echo.

His thinking was slower than his eyes, but the word came back to him: tent, he was in a tent, an almost-familiar branch-and-hide structure curving overhead.

He was in a tent. And awake. Alive. Yes. The thought surprised him, but he didn't know why. He had been asleep. For... a long time, he thought. Had he been ill?

"Ill and then some, Listens to Two Voices."

That was... not his name. But he would not dare say that to the woman who now knelt beside him. He had not heard her arrive any more than he had heard the boy leave, and he thought vaguely that should worry him. Instead, he studied her. She was ancient, the boy's oak-hued skin replaced by the gnarls of willow, folded and creased until she looked as though she might shatter in a strong wind.

Tent. Elder.

He tried to remember how he had come to be here and could not. The last thing, the only thing he remembered was pain, urgency, and water.

Water. He flinched, half-expecting to feel the sluice of water against his skin, dripping from wet hair and clothing. But the weight of a blanket over him was dry, his skin fire-parched, his scalp itchy from dirt.

Instinct made him reach out, told him there was water nearby; a rushing stream, tumbling over rocks and pooling, full of fish. There was an odd feeling at knowing that, satisfaction mingled with sadness. In the States, that awareness had been muted, bearable. Ergo, he was no longer in the States, logic confirming what instinct had already told him.

The States. Philadelphia.

Gone now, beyond his reach.

Dry lips cracked painfully, until he tasted blood on his tongue.

"Grandmother," he said, testing the word out, and he would have winced at the raven's croak his voice had become, although he could not have sworn what it sounded like before. His fingers moved in tradespeak, restless against the weave of the blanket. "Where am I?"

She placed a hard hand on his bare chest, fingers spread, and pressed down. "Home," she said. "You have come home, Two Voices. Now sleep, and heal."

He had no home. He wanted to argue with her, to question, but with that hand on him, he had no choice. He slept. And in the morning, he rose, and returned to life.

But he did not heal. Not entirely.

2

The Territory, Now.

IT WAS past dusk when the man realized that it was dusk, that day had come and gone and he had no idea what had become of it, or where it had even begun.

Who, an owl called out overhead. His head turned, tracking its flight slowly, cautiously, as though he were one of the meadow-things it might hunt.

"Who?" the bird asked again, and then responded, "*you.*"

"Me," the man said, but the word held no more meaning than the owl's cry, the word dry and empty on his tongue. He could recall no name, no sense of self to pin on his flesh.

He looked down, seeing a flint striker in his hands, a small pile of kindling set within rocks in front of him. That was what he had been doing when the owl distracted him: making a fire. Yes.

His body knew what actions to take, and yet it took too long for the fire to catch, his hands stiff and chilled, reluctant to bend or turn. The flint seemed equally reluctant to spark; the kindling branches gathered into a square reluctant to burn despite their crackling dryness.

It was him, his fault. He was rain and river, creek and spring, and fire fled from him as though he might douse it.

The thought surprised him, bitter and brackish-tasting. He looked down at his hands again, half-expecting them to flow blue-clear and liquid rather than bone and flesh. But he saw only skin under the rising moonlight, pale and rough. The nails were ragged but the beds below were clean, as though they'd never been dirtied or bloodied before.

They had been. Often. Recently.

Who? an echo of the owl asked, and he could not answer. He felt no alarm at the absence, merely accepted it as he accepted the flint in his hand and the kindling in front of him, and the owl and the moon overhead. He was. They were. Facts. You could not dismiss facts, only argue them into meaningless-ness. Someone had told him that once, someone...

Memory danced just out of reach. *Let it go,* a whisper told him.

He let it go.

He flexed the fingers holding the flint, watching the knuck-lebones shift. Water and bones. The words meant something, but he could not recall that, either. He flexed his fingers again, watched the skin draw tight, deep creases and needle-thick scars turned white by age.

Behind him something heavy moved, and he stilled even as a sense deeper within him recognized it as not-a-threat, famil-iar, belonging.

Horse. The warm shape moving behind him was a horse. His mind's eye described the gelding without having to look back, its square head and low haunch, along with the knowing that the horse was his, and that it would alert him if danger came from behind.

The horse was his. He was not alone. That thought focused

his hands enough to strike tinder properly, a tiny red spark dropping onto the kindling, and he cradled the infant flame until it spread, placing larger pieces of kindling in a pattern until they caught in turn, then carefully placing small branches around it, gauging the proper moment to place more over the flame until the fire leapt up, embracing the fuel and settling itself into a steady blaze.

The crackle and hiss was a welcome sound, and he held his hands out to the flame, letting warmth slowly return. How long had he been cold? Not long, not because the cold felt like a new thing, but because there was no damage to his hands, no numbness to his face or skin. He glanced up, away from the firelight, and let the moonlight reveal that here was no snow around him. The air was chill, and the ground underfoot still frozen, but he was not at risk for frostbite so long as he kept dry and near the fire. These facts slotted neatly into place, reassuringly solid.

But he knew, too, that he had been damp. No, not damp, sodden to the skin, clothing drip-heavy, and he shivered in revulsion. He had been soaked, drenched, water in his nose and ears as though he'd been submerged—

A wave of nausea roiled through him, salted bile filling his mouth.

Let it come and let it go a voice said again, and he thought for a crazed instant it had been the horse before another memory returned. Years before, his mouth filled with muddy water and his body wracked with fever, and the medicine woman who had walked him out of the river.

Old Woman Who Never Dies.

And as though the medicine woman had placed her hands on him once again, he remembered himself.

His horse, Steady, was behind him, and the fire was before him, and his name was Gabriel. Gabriel Kasun, also known to some as Two Voices.

And he had left Isobel in Red Stick.

That memory struck him like a sharp blow, bending him forward at the waist, and he twisted his fingers at the back of his head, tangling in his hair as though to yank the stands out by the root. He was Gabriel Kasun, mentor to the Devil's Hand, and he had abandoned her to whatever was coming, to the unrest that was rising in the city of Red Stick, left her without a word of warning or explanation.

The facts were unchangeable. They had been in Red Stick. He had brought them there for what should have been winter quarters, a place for Isobel to rest and recover after nearly a year of riding the Road, learning how to be the Devil's Left Hand, learning the powers she had Bargained herself for.

Instead, they had ridden directly into unrest and rumor, the sickness that seemed to be spreading throughout the Territory, bubbling there like pus under a wound. And Isobel had been driven by her Bargain to be the blade that lanced it, the silver that cleansed it.

It was what she did. It was what she *was*. But he should have been by her side, at her back, ready to lend whatever support she needed. He was her mentor, her guardian, her teacher.

Instead, he had left her without a word, had ridden to the edge of the river, the Mudwater, and...

And done what? What had happened once he got there?

The gap of memory remained, red-hazed and terrifying, and he stepped back from it, not yet ready to look deeper.

Let it come and let it go.

The medicine woman's words brought no comfort this time. Whatever his reasons, he had abandoned Isobel.

Never mind that she was well-set to deal with the situation, that she was the only one who *was* set to deal with it; never mind that he had known when they rode into Red Stick that he'd taught her and taken her as far as he could. Never mind that he had not left her alone, that the marshal was with her, that the river-witch was with her. He had still left her without a word, without a warning, driven by his own weakness and fear, and he had no sense of how much time had passed since then.

That thought brought his head up sharply. "Where *am* I, anyway?"

A Rider's sense of the Territory, once learned, was a map constantly unfolding in their head, the feel of the Road underneath their boots a steady, reassuring presence. But here...he could feel none of that.

Slowly, firmly, he stilled his panic. There were yet places in the Territory where the Road did not travel, the weight of human passage light enough not to have pressed a trail for others to follow. But this close to Red Stick, he was surprised not to at least feel it nearby...

But he did not in fact know that he was close to Red Stick; he had no idea how long he had been outside himself.

Facts. He needed more facts.

Rising to his feet, Gabriel looked around more carefully, taking note of his surroundings. He had made rough camp in a shallow meadow, gear piled to one side of the fire, a crude circle drawn in salt marking the site, invoking hospitality and rider protections. He hadn't been so far out of his mind, then, that he'd forgotten basic skills, or survival. He supposed that was a good thing.

There was a hill rising directly to his left, the grass silvered under the moon and starlight, a ridge of trees standing sentinel halfway up, where the owl had flown. To his right and front, the meadow sloped gently before rising again. And behind him...

He took a deep breath before turning to look.

It took him a moment to find it, but the wide, flat ribbon of the Mudwater lay behind him, glimmering in the moonlight, distant enough that he thought there must be two, three days steady ride between them. Red Stick itself, its high wooden walls, was hidden again in one of the endless curves, devil alone knew how far downriver.

There was no sign of the Road, or even a half-broken track to tell him how he had arrived at this place. No sign of anything save the fire he'd built, and the salt circle he'd laid down.

Hesitant, as though half-expecting a rebuke or worse, to hear nothing at all, he calmed his breathing, eased his too-tight muscles, and let himself reach for the Road. It was nothing he had not done a thousand or more times in his lifetime, had taught others to do, had done as naturally as breathing. It would not mean anything if there was silence, would not mean that his connection to the Territory had been cut, and if it had, it would be nothing more than he'd once begged for.

Despite that, he did not draw breath until an answering touch came, the scrape of warm rock against skin. It was distant, muted, telling him nothing more than what he had already determined, that he had ridden north and west of Red Stick, away from the Mudwater.

Away from Isobel.

Guilt dug claws into his chest, but with it also came a sense of sick relief. With the distance he'd traveled, there was no going back. Whatever had happened was done, and if she had succeeded or failed, it was her story now, not his.

He had discharged his obligation. He owed nothing to anyone.

You would be in my debt, if you did this, the devil had said that day in Flood, when he'd offered to take on a Greenie girl with the strong-boned face and fine eyes.

But there was no debt. There was no binding on him, that the devil could yank. While Gabriel might have ridden into the town of Flood thinking to test himself against the Master of the Territory, in the end he had not wanted anything the devil had to offer. His offer to mentor that young girl had been made not to the devil but Isobel herself, free of cost; that the Old Man had accepted on her behalf should not change that.

He had done as he had promised when he offered to take an uncertain, ambitious child on the Road and teach her how to survive. He owed nothing more, and nothing was owed to him.

And Isobel herself?

Something made the corner of his lip tick up, in what almost might have been a smile. The Road connected back to itself, eventually. She would rail at him when they encountered each other again, but he thought mayhap she would forgive him. Eventually.

If she survived.

That made the smile disappear, and he pressed a clenched fist against his chest, hard enough the bone underneath ached.

She lived. He knew it, once he thought to ask, rock-solid and certain. Isobel was too deeply a part of the Territory now to disappear unnoticed.

"Thank you," he whispered to whatever had brought him that news, and let his hand fall back down to his side, crouching again by the fire to feed it again, one stick at a time.

The flames took his offering with fresh crackling, smoke curling around the fuel before rising into the air and fading into the night, a faint heat-haze. He rested his hands on his knees, sitting back on his haunches. He could feel himself, heavy in his own flesh again, solid and real.

And alone.

"That's that, then. Back to my own self. Riding solo."

There was a heavy huffing noise behind him, and a warm, rough-whiskered nose bumped against the back of his head, attempting to mouth at his hair as though offended at being forgotten. He reached back to push the horse away, and chuckled. "Sorry. Solo con caballo."

He would need to check Steady's hooves in the morning, make sure he'd taken no damage in those days Gabriel could not remember. And check his saddlebags, see what supplies he had with him. The day he'd ridden out of Red Stick he'd packed out of habit, not thinking he would need anything. He hadn't thought he would be gone long... and halfway had not expected to return at all.

That admission was bitter as grass. He'd gone to face the Mudwater, knowing full-well what that meant. He'd given up.

They'd ridden into the southeastern Territory because Isobel needed to know it, needed to know Red Stick with its mass of peoples, its significance in terms of trade and defense. He'd managed to not think about the fact that it sat at the mouth of the Mudwater itself until the river began to whisper to him. Asleep, waking, it did not cajole, it did not threaten, it merely reminded him with every breath he took that it was there. That it waited for him, as it had been waiting for years.

What water cannot move, it wears down. Human flesh could be no match for it.

He had gone to Grandmother River and shouted at her. Had admitted defeat, had given up, had gone knee-deep in the muddy waters and...

What had happened after that still hid from him, wrapped in fog and smudges.

Gabriel knew he should unroll his kit, stop thinking, try to get some sleep. Instead he sat by the fire, occasionally feeding another piece of wood into the flames, and listened to the susurration of insects in the grass around him, the distant hoot of an owl still hunting, until his eyes slid shut under their own weight.

The water had lapped at his toes, brackish-brown, not the red of his walking-dreams, the familiar stink of rotting logs settling at the base of his nostrils. He felt the weight of the river reach out and up, an unrelenting roll that would take and drown him, if he let it.

It was a dream. Gabriel knew that, familiar after all these years with the varying tastes of dreams, the cool mint of being dreamwalked, the sour citrus of a spirit-animal's intrusion, the sharp pepper of an ordinary dream. This was none of those, the dank salt identifying it as memory come back in different form to haunt him.

Twenty years before, when he'd first left the Territory, had *tried* to leave the Territory and been driven back, forced to abandon the life he'd begun there, the future he'd planned. What the Territory claimed it did not let go. And so, he'd returned, stumbling and sick and nearly dead, to let the river have him.

Instead, he'd woken in a Hochunk camp under the care of their medicine woman. She'd pulled him from the waters, had cleared the mud from his lungs and walked with him until his legs remembered how to stand on their own.

Her people called her Old Woman Who Never Dies. She had named him Hears Two Voices and told him he could not run from himself.

She had told him many things, most of which he'd promptly ignored, burying himself under resignation and inevitability, under the knowledge that the Territory was stronger than he, would always be stronger, and that the only fight he could win would be the refusal to let it own him entirely.

He'd taken the horse they'd given him and taken to the Road, thinking that if he only kept moving, he would be all right. The Territory might claim him, but it could not *have* him. The medicine of the bones, the magic of the crossroads, the whispers of the water in his veins, he kept it all at bay, using only what he must, and no more.

He'd lived that way for years.

But seeing Isobel grow into her Bargain, the toll that tying herself to the Territory took but also the strength she gained from it, the sense of *herself* she seemed to gain, had sprouted doubt in the kernel of his stubbornness, the tentative thought that the Territory need not be adversary.

But still, he could not give in. To even think of it sent the taste of bile to his mouth, dropped a stone against his heart. He could not forgive, and he could not forget.

And then they had ridden into Red Stick, and for the first time in years, he heard not the gentle whispers of the creeks and streams, but the endless voice of Grandmother River herself. Implacable. Unending.

Heal, Old Woman had told him.

He'd tried. But in that moment, he realized that all he'd done was manage not to die.

"Have done with me!"

He had shouted the words not in anger nor fear, but with the voice of a man who had gone as far as he could, until the rope of his mortality caught him, and he could strain no more. He had stood at the banks and stared into the brackish waters, his voice breaking. "Have done with me, Grandmother River. Either let me go or drown me, once and for all."

He had tried to escape once and failed, the nightmare of that desperate journey buried deep, refusing and resisting and denying to the devil's face that he was broken.

Gabriel Kasun. Two Voices. Rider. There was nothing he did not have that he wanted.

Except his freedom.

Twenty years and countless miles later, Gabriel gave in.

He had waited, the waters lapping at his toes, mud sucking at his heels. The sounds of insects and birds and fish slapping the water had been quieter than the silence as he waited for a response that never came, damp chill settling on his skin, seeping into his flesh.

"You called me, and finally, finally, I came. And now you shut me out? Have *done!*"

"Have done!"

Gabriel woke with a start, the words rising from a rubbed-sore throat, startling a pair of deer that had been grazing just beyond the fading firelight. They dashed off a few paces, then stopped, looking back at him before disappearing into the shadows.

He forced himself to breathe, inhaling deeply and then exhaling slowly until the fluttering panic subsided and he was back firmly within his own flesh again. The fire crackled warm at his front, the air was night-cool and still on his skin, and in the leaps and crackles of the flames, he thought he heard the spice-warm, mockingly affectionate voice of the Master of the Territory asking him if he'd truly thought it would be that easy. If shouting had ever solved anything.

"Damn you all, anyway," he grumbled into the night. "Graciendo had been right."

Old Bear had warned him not to form attachments, to keep himself apart from others, to not linger overlong or care overmuch. He'd been fine with his life until Isobel. Not perfect, not content, but fine.

He had been born with water sense—dowsing, they called it back East. Water-child, the witch in Red Stick had called him. He could feel the flow of fresh water, be it deep under his feet or running the surface of the Territory. The Touch, folk called it. The hand of the Territory on those who were born within its borders, its medicine born deep in their bones.

Nobody had warned him, when he left to study at the Eastern universities. Nobody had told him what would happen, the blood-sick that would near kill him.

He had come back, then. He had learned to love the rolling plains and deep forests, the dry deserts and snow-capped rises again. But he had never forgiven it.

And the devil had known all that when he entered the saloon in Flood, when he sat down across the desk from him. He had promised Gabriel freedom when he was done.

But if the devil never lied, neither was he obligated to tell all the truth, and Gabriel wondered now what sort of fool he had been to think it would be that simple. The devil might protect the Territory, but he did not control it. "Master" was a title others gave the devil for the need to have someone to blame.

And yet. And yet. The devil did not lie.

Alone in the night, Gabriel's thought scrambled for scraps, flitting like a flock of butterflies in the wind, stars fluttering just past his fingertips. The devil was master in name only. And yet Territory allowed his pronouncements to stand, allowed his Hands to shape its magic, touch deeper than Gabriel had ever seen, had heard stories of. The River and the Knife lent the devil their strengths, that he might hold the borders against ill-intent.

They were connected, the devil and the Territory, guardians and their magics, in some way no mortal understood. The devil might not tell all the truth, but neither did he lie.

Gabriel was owed his freedom.

In his dream—no, in *fact*, in *memory*—he had stood at the banks and faced Grandmother River, had challenged her, and through her, the Territory itself. Had asked —demanded—that they let him be.

He... had stepped into the water, felt the mud squelch at his heels, grab at his legs. Had seen the maw of something rise from the swirling depths, a single great eye looking at him.

But he could remember no more. He could not remember if they had answered.

"All right, then," he said quietly. "All right then."

Gabriel was afraid, but he'd been afraid for years, and one more moment would not break him more. Inhaling deeply, he reached inward, gathering himself, then reached out as he'd not done since he was a child, allowing that water-sense to flow through him, giving it permission just this once more for it to rule him.

Awareness of the Territory spread out before him in hues of blue-green and white: the still water resting deep under his feet, the creeklet running through the grass north of him, the moisture hanging heavy in the sky above, and underneath it all, the faint, waiting thrum of the greater rivers, a near-silent rumble he could feel in his soul.

Gabriel pulled away, breaking the connection, wrapping himself up tightly again, near-shaking with the effort.

There was no freedom there. Nothing had changed. Whatever had happened when he confronted the Mudwater, whatever had crept within him, nothing of *him* had changed.

The Territory had not relinquished its claim.

Bitterness tainted his tongue and filled his nose, something ugly scrabbling with poisoned claws at his throat, the smell and feel of mud coating hands, water weighing down his clothes.

The only freedom the devil had given him was the freedom from hope he hadn't realized he'd still had.

Gabriel ran the fingers of one hand through his hair, tugging at the ends in frustration. But why then had his memory of the confrontation been fogged? Why had he not returned to town, to Isobel, but instead ridden away?

"Did you mean to do that, or was it simply carelessness? Punishment? Did you wait all those years for me to bend a knee, only to take your revenge? Did my suffering amuse you?"

Gabriel let his words die in the air. The Mudwater could not hear him and would not respond even if it did.

There was no such thing as freedom, despite what his younger self had believed; something always tied you down, with or without your consent.

"So, what now? You've cut me loose but not let me go. What now?"

The insects sang and the fire crackled, and he rolled his eyes, although he was not sure if it was at the Territory's silence, or his own half-expectation of a reply.

Giving up, he banked the fire properly, then unrolled his kit and lay down. The ground was uneven, the blankets cold, and his body felt unpleasantly itchy, keeping him from rest. Instead, he watched as the stars turned and faded, the full disc of the moon casting a paler light against the ground as it too began to retreat.

Off to the side, Steady made an unhappy groaning noise in his sleep, and Gabriel wondered if the horse missed his companions. Flatfoot had been with them for several years, but he had left the mule at the stable with Isobel's mare, Uvnee, along with most of their belongings. Taking to the road unprepared, without supplies or stock, was incredibly foolish—the act of a Greenie fresh out of the schoolroom—and being mind-fogged was no excuse. If Isobel had done such a thing, no matter the reason, he would have lectured her for a week. And yet... he felt no regret, no panic, not even the slightest worry about what was to come. Nor did he feel defeated or bitter, despite the regrets that dogged him.

He felt... light.

"Lightheaded, mayhap," he grumbled to himself, and pulled the blanket further over his shoulders, forcing his eyes to close until the first tendrils of sunlight finally reached over the valley, brightening the shadows.

Gabriel rubbed his eyes with the back of one hand, knowing without looking that they were red-rimmed with exhaustion. Traveling alone in such a state was foolish, but there was a feeling in his bones like striking flint, making him twitch with the need to be gone from here.

Once he reached the Road again, things would make more sense.

Sitting up, he reached for his boots, shaking them out to make sure nothing had taken refuge overnight, then pulled them on, pressing his heels into the dirt to make sure they settled properly. "At least no pack means nothing to load." It also meant nothing to cook for breakfast, but the tightness in his stomach suggested he wanted nothing to do with food just yet. By the time it unknotted, he should have come to a farm or steading where he could trade for supplies with the coin he had on him And if not... well, he had his carbine and his knife, and there were always rabbits or pheasant for the trapping. His father and grandfather would rise as haints if he shamed them by starving to death.

His shirt felt stiff with sweat and dirt, but a quick whiff of his arm told him he had another day or so before he became objectionable, and it wasn't as though Steady was likely to complain.

"We'll feel better once we've the Road under us again," he told the horse, checking each hoof for stones or cracks, then running a flat hand across his back, checking to make sure there were no burrs or lumps before tossing the saddle on and tightening the belly strap. The horse dropped its head to eye him, as though judging the veracity of his words, and then sighed, his flanks huffing against the band before accepting the inevitable.

The banked fire had mostly burnt itself out by the time he was ready to go; it was a simple matter of stomping the ash underfoot until the last faint glimmer of red died to grey, and then splashing water from his canteen—suspiciously full—over the remains. He waited to make sure it was out—he'd seen too many grassfires to ever be careless —before kicking the fire circle apart, scattering the rocks back into the grass. Odds were low there would be another traveler passing this way any time soon; there was no reason to leave it in place.

His long coat had been folded over the saddle with his usual, wide-brimmed hat placed neatly on top, woolen gloves stuffed into the deep pockets. He shrugged into the coat, fitting the brimmed hat securely on his head, but left the gloves where they were. Winters this far south were mild compared to what fell in the north, but the weight of the weathered sheepskin felt good in the morning chill, and he could always take it off later if need be.

A quick check of the carbine and powder, and they were both latched into place on the saddle before he swung up onto Steady's back, feeling the horse settle under his weight. Some of the scraping sensation in his bones subsided as his legs pressed against the gelding's side, feeling the slide of the leather reins through his fingers.

Gabriel turned his back pointedly on the direction he'd come from and considered his options. For the first time in nearly a year, he had nothing weighing on his choices, no place he should be and nothing and no-one waiting on his decisions.

That was as close to freedom as he'd ever known.

He closed his eyes, and breathed in, nostrils flaring as though to test the winds. The Road looped in on itself, never-ending, but the road you chose shaped the journey you took.

East beyond the River was closed to him, and to the south lay nothing but regret. All the way west was the Mother's Knife, the mountain range that kept the Spaniards from them, where living silver was pulled from the stones, and Graciendo kept his cabin. But too many memories lay there, both good and bad, waiting to drop like a rope around his neck.

North, all the way north lay the place where he had been born, and beyond that the Wilds, where a man could lose himself for a lifetime—or die within a day. But it was also deepest winter there, and the passes would be closed to any sane man or beast.

"Somewhere dry," he decided. "Somewhere empty, where the riverbeds can only whisper, and the bones lay close to the sun."

West and north, then, into the high desert plains.

3

He'd been right: once he could feel the Road again, could find himself on the living map of the territory, his mood improved, and his thoughts cleared.

"Pity those stuck behind wards and walls, never seeing more than the same horizon, day after day," Gabriel told Steady, leaning forward on the saddle horn and cocking his hat against the sun's glare. He'd lived in cities, ones far more crowded than Red Stick had been, but after so many years on the Road, he could not breathe freely unless the land spread open in front of him. There were no awkward questions, no uncomfortable demands here, only the sky and the soil and the steady beat of hooves and heart in tandem.

The air was still bright and crisp with winter's bite, but there were hints of green dotting the long stretches of bare shrubs and brown soil around them. Under the pale blue sky, a pair of carrion-birds circled, their silhouettes too high above for them to be seriously considering anything on the ground. A few yards ahead, three mule deer bounded across their path, pausing only long enough to give them a considering glance before disappearing into the shoulder-high seed-tips. He opened his mouth to ask Isobel if she knew the legend about Mule Deer and Coyote, before remembering.

That hadn't been the first time he'd done that. Years of riding alone, or with temporary companions, had been washed away after three seasons of regular company and conversation.

Fortunately, Steady had never minded listening to him ramble, adding an ear twitch or snort at intervals only he understood.

"Think we should follow them? Think they know where they're going?"

The road they'd been riding had narrowed that morning, slowly fading into nothing more than a rutted track through the grasslands, slanting up and up along gently rolling hills. If the deer knew a shorter way through, perhaps they should take it.

The thought made him laugh, rubbing the back of his hand against his chin, feeling rough, sweat-sticky stubble. Once, he would never have left the track, preferring even the faint protection it gave against the risk of encountering something lurking within the grasses. Demon or bear, or merely a wind looking to cause mischief. Or a magician...

"With luck, we're of no interest to any of them," he told Steady, who didn't even bother flickering an ear back this time to prove he was listening. Riding with Isobel, he'd learned to brace himself for such encounters. Not bears so much, but things of power were drawn to her, hungry moths to a bright-burning flame. He'd seen more in those months than any sane man would fear. Without her, though, he was barely a flicker, one of a thousand or more throughout the Territory.

"And I'm fine with that," he said out loud, in case any lingering wind or skulking demon might decide to prove him wrong. He touched his left hand to the silver of his belt buckle, its gleaming brightness a reassurance that no magician worked their mischief nearby. Demon and spirit creatures were one thing, a manageable thing, but those who bartered themselves to the winds gained power at the cost of all their sense. "If you see a magician, run," was advice given to every child, with reason.

Although not all were mindless menaces. Entirely.

"Jordan wash whatever was left of your soul, and keep it far from me," he murmured to the memory of Farron Easterly, who had traveled with them briefly before dying, once and then again, until it—Gabriel assumed—had finally taken. He had feared the magician, and pitied him, a little. Respected him, maybe, just a bit. But he did not miss him, at all.

He missed Isobel, a little. More than any other he'd mentored. But it grew easier each day to wake alone.

Graciendo had been right: it was easier to be alone.

In the end, he kept Steady's hooves on the path, faint though it was, heading due west. There were occasional farmsteads in the distance, but he kept clear of them. The seed-tips were low enough here that he could beat down a nest of sorts each night, using the flickering remains of his coalstone for light rather than risking open flame. He set traps before sleeping, occasionally catching a rabbit or grass-hen, cooking what he could eat that day and leaving the rest, raw, for less-lucky predators to find when he broke camp.

And if he sometimes sat up under the stars and listened for owls, asking *who, who, you,* that was nobody's business but his own.

After about a week of that, even the faint track ran out, just about the same time the tall grasses gave way to shorter growths, and then stretches of low spotted brush and yellowish soil. The sun wasn't any brighter, but the air felt warmer. Black-brown chaparral birds dashed underfoot, and when the crescent moon rose, he heard the song of coyote singing, each to each. Save for the smudge of greenish gray against the horizon where mountains lurked, in that moment, the entire of the Territory was him, his horse, and the spray of stars overhead.

Part of him wanted nothing more than to continue until he could no longer find his way back, until the sun and moon were one and the same, and he fell into the hole Badger left when he dug up the mountains. But while rabbits and grass-hens were plentiful enough to keep the edge off his own hunger, there was only so long a man could live on bloody meat, and winter grasses were not enough to keep Steady healthy. They were going to need supplies sooner rather than later. And that meant finding a town, or at very least, a farm-stead with enough surplus that they could share some with a needy, foolish Rider.

With that in mind, when he saw a building in the distance one morning, a pale hint of a structure breaking the horizon, he turned Steady toward it, more out of hope than any real expec-tation of success.

The closer they came, the less hope it gave him. While a battered road came from behind, and curved around past it, heading back north, there seemed little indication that anyone had traveled by recently, and the red-brown walls of the building itself gave no sign of life. There was a second, low-roofed building off to the side that might have been a stable, and a small garden half-hidden under poles and cloth, but no other sign of vitality.

But a closer look told another story. Both buildings had been set at an angle to avoid even the hint of a crossroad, a boulder seemingly dropped in the middle of the road in front of the main building and painted with sigils to divert anything that might try to flow along it. Someone had put a great deal of thought and effort into ensuring that the Territory's power slid gently past, rather than pooling as a beacon for magicians, or others bent on mischief. Gabriel approved.

As though taunting him for his lack of expectations, a

weather-worn painted sign over the building's door proclaimed that it was a mercantile.

"If there's a seller, there must be buyers as well," he told Steady. It seemed unlikely, but to be fair, he'd seen thriving towns grow from less.

"Odds to evens, three or five years from now they'll have a badgehouse and a dressmaker and mayhap even a teashop," he said, pulling Steady to a soft halt. "But let's go see what they have now, hey?"

There was a single posting rail set against the front, and he looped Steady's reins loosely around it. He'd no worries the horse might spook—anything four— or no—legged that came near his hooves the gelding would smash into the dust, and he doubted anyone was lurking behind the garden, intent on theft.

He pulled the topmost saddlebag off its ties and slung it over his shoulder. What little coin he had was in there, and also items he might be able to use for trade. His hand rested on the stock of his carbine for a moment, then dropped to the knife sheathed against his leg. If there was a threat inside, the time it took to load the carbine meant it would be near-useless save as a club, anyway.

The door was set at ground level, the wood planed smoother than expected, swinging inward on near-silent hinges. Gabriel felt his skin prickle as he went from sunlight into shadows, too aware that he was silhouetted perfectly in the doorway.

Inside the mercantile it was blessedly cool, the few windows placed high for light, and swung open to allow warm air to escape, and the shelves were as sparse of merchandise as he'd anticipated.

"Buenos tardes, señor," a voice came from the shadows.

"Buenos tardes," Gabriel replied, squinting a little to get a better look at the man who had greeted him. Slight and short, his shirtsleeves rolled up past the elbow, and a mustache that twitched as he spoke, Gabriel was put in mind of a weasel more than a man, and the combination of isolation and appearance set his spine upright, his fingers curving around the hilt of his knife.

"What may I do for you, what may I do indeed?" The mustache seemed to have almost a life of his own, twitching over the patter that fell from the storekeeper' mouth. "We're far from civilization as you can see, and my normal custom is more a settler seeking a length of pretty cloth or a bag of flour, or one of our locals seeking to trade furs for powder or sweets. Not none such as you, Rider, no indeed. What may I do for you this fine day?"

The words were smooth, but there was something about the man that rubbed Gabriel rough. He had been born the woods of the northern wilds, spent more than half his life wandering the Territory, and before matching with Isobel, he'd never seen a spirit animal, had encountered only a handful of demon, and never once faced a magician. But he needed none of those experiences, only the clench in his gut, to tell him that this mercantile-keeper was nothing human.

As unobtrusively as possible, he loosened the tie holding his knife in the sheath, checking the silver to see if it had begun to tarnish. A faint darkening of the metal confirmed his suspicions.

"If you seek to trap me in wishes, you should keep a closer watch on your tongue," he told it. "A man woken to suspicion is a man harder to beguile."

"But a man sharp with his words drives a more interesting bargain," the mercantile-keeper said, and when he spoke, he no longer tried to hide the fur-tufted ears, or the pale gold of his eyes. "And you're more interesting than most."

Like most riders, Gabriel had trained his memory to recall details of the places he'd been, the people he'd encountered, and the dangers endemic to the Dust Roads. But he could not recall, standing there, every hearing of a being with ears and eyes like those. But there was more hidden in the Territory than was known even by the native tribes, and much of what they knew, they did not tell outsiders.

Another quick check of the silver on his knife and belt buckle showed no further tarnish: whatever this creature was, it was offering no immediate threat. Gabriel lifted his hand away, but kept the blade untied in warning.

"I've traded words with the devil himself," he told it carefully, "and won his regard. I've no desire to make further bargain."

The creature's eyes widened, dark lashes sweeping down almost coyly. "Phoo. And you the only interesting thing that's come along in days. Are you sure you won't play, even a little bit?"

The mockery was real, but so was the disappointment, and Gabriel eased back just a hair. Whatever it might call itself, Gabriel knew a Trickster when he met one. Every story said they were dangerous if crossed or insulted, but if Gabriel behaved himself, so too would the other.

"Afraid not," he said. "Just came in to replenish my supplies."

"What then may I sell you, O Rider, that this visit not be an entire waste for us both?"

Not dangerous, no, but the creature was not to be trusted, either. A wise man would make his excuses and leave without buying anything, give the creature no chance to do... anything. But Gabriel had ridden with the Devil's Hand and learned that on occasion wisdom was the same as being foolish.

"I'm traveling light these days," he said, instead. "Hunting when I've need, sleeping under the stars and over the dirt." He could use another pan, and dried fruit, and a tuck of molasses would be welcome. But his coin was limited, and he had to choose carefully. "I could use a new coalstone, if you've one on hand. A handclasp of dried beans, and a bag of dry mash. And gut-string, to replace my fishing line."

"Ahhh, coalstone, coalstone." The being clapped its hands together and turned to survey the store as though the object might appear from nowhere. "Coalstone, beans, mash, and.... gut-string, Nahshon! Get out here. Where do we keep those things?"

"Left drawer, bottom cabinet, and the top shelf, left cabinet." The voice seemed to come from nowhere, then one of the larger cabinet doors against the far wall opened and the brim of a black hat emerged, then a face, covered in the sparse hair of a young man, followed by a lanky body, a canvas apron folded over at his waist. "The same places they've been since forever."

"Forever is a very long time," the Trickster said, pulling open a drawer and poking inside. "It's longer even than always. You've run a long way, but you've still a long way to go before that."

Gabriel froze. "What do you mean?"

The grin the Trickster gave him had far too many teeth, more than it had had a moment ago. "You can always run, but you can't run forever."

The second man pushed at his shoulder and pointed to the drawer next to the one he'd opened. "Take Mouse-Face with some salt, Rider. He's a terrible person, and should never be allowed to talk to anyone, but for all that, reasonably honest."

"You're cruel to me," Mouse-Face retorted, clutching a red-clawed hand to his chest. "Terribly cruel."

"Because I said you were terrible, or because I said you were honest?" While the other figure seemed to be pondering their answer, Nahshon shifted around him, going to another cabinet and opening it, taking down a tin box.

"One coalstone." He placed the box on the counter, then squinted at it as though calculating its worth. "Two silver? Two silver coin seems fair."

"Two coins is high-road robbery," Gabriel said, shaking his head and settling in for a bargaining session. "Half a coin, at most. And another coin for the rest."

"You are the one who needs, we are the one who has," Mouse-Face interjected, abandoning insult and offense, and the opened drawers, for the lure of bargaining. "Three silver, and I'll throw in a new kerchief, for yours is a disgrace."

Gabriel eyed him cautiously. "I'll take the kerchief and give you two coin for it all."

Mouse-Face's ears twitched, and this time his upset seemed real. "Rider, you seek to ruin me!"

"Pfah, you're both enough to give a worm a stomach ache," Nashon said in disgust, leaving the box to duck into the cabinet again and coming out with a flat packet of fish string. "Two and a half coin for all, and you'll both go away unhappy, but I'll be happy that you've gone."

"The store's yours, not his," Gabriel realized.

"It is," Nashon said. "Mouse-Face showed up one day, and despite my best encouragement has never left. But it allows me to study during the daylight hours, saving candles, while he deals with our occasional customers. It amuses him, I think, to play merchant."

"You'd have died your first week here, without me," Mouse-Face grumbled. "You and all your scholarly fools. Settling where there's nothing but dreams and nightmares."

Nashon seemed unbothered by the accusation. "Dreams are what make us live. And nightmares may be banished."

"Bah." Mouse-Face waved the man's words away. "A barn of fools, while chickens sleep in your beds and eat your corn."

Gabriel had been among madmen before, but never so well-spoken. Nor ones who squabbled like an old married couple. Nashon seemed mortal enough, but what business had brought him here and tangled him with the likes of a trickster —a trickster that seemed to have taken in his people, too...?

There was a story there no doubt, and another day Gabriel might have been interested in learning it, but the Trickster's odd words earlier lingered, and he'd no desire to find out what else it might decide to say to him. "Two and a half coin it is," he said, dropping the silver bits on the counter and scooping up his purchases, barely noticed as the two continued to bicker. "And a pleasant day to you both."

OUTSIDE AGAIN, Gabriel looked up at the pale blue sky overhead, a slip of grey-white cloud now drifting across it and shook his head. "You'd have been fascinated by those two," he said to the companion no longer at his side. "And they probably would have loved you." Isobel had drawn the uncanny to her, sensing the power she carried. Not that that was always a good thing, and he kicked himself for not warning her about mischief-makers like Mouse-Face.

He hoped she was being cautious, that he'd taught her well enough to be wary, but there was nothing he could do for it now; she either would or she would not, and if she would not... Well, the Left Hand could handle herself. He had confidence in that much, at least.

He replaced the saddlebag, now holding the fishing line and coalstone, and tied the sacks holding the mash and beans to the leather hooks ready at the back of the saddle, checking how they hung before unhitching Steady from the post and swinging back up into the saddle. The new kerchief, a cheerful swatch of red fabric, he tied around his head in an attempt to keep too-shaggy hair out of his face before replacing his hat on top.

Ready to ride out once more, he considered the road that looped around the store. It was not well-trod, true, and Mouse-Face had said not many came along, but it was more and better than he'd seen in days of travel. If he followed it, he might come upon where Nashon's kin lived, mayhap even a settlement.

He looked up into the sky, squinting into the sun, and then turned his back on the road, and headed back out into the emptiness again.

Two weeks later, Gabriel was beginning to regret his choice. He might have wanted silence and solitude, but there had been sight nor sign of another human being since he left the mercantile, not even the remains of a hunting camp, and he had reached a point where even a demon might be welcome company, if only to have something to speak to that spoke back.

Other than the horse and himself, the terrain was deserted. Occasionally a raptor soared overhead, searching for one of the same rabbits Gabriel hunted, or the carcass of a half-eaten deer left to bloat under the sun. But it was winter, and game here was scarce; if he couldn't catch a rabbit soon, or find a creek with fish in it, he'd be reduced to insects and grubs. They weren't the worst things he'd ever eaten, but they would do little to fill his belly, or keep his thinking sharp. His boots and clothes were coated in dust, and there was little water to spare for washing; he was able to break moisture from nopale paddles, letting the juice sit in his mouth before swallowing, but it was too sticky to use for anything else. He'd passed other edible plants, but either their fruit grew too high for easy gathering, or they were protected by thorns that would have taken too long to remove.

He was not a man to take offense easily, but it was almost as though the Territory itself had decided to make his self-imposed isolation as difficult as possible.

"You're still with me, though, right Steady? Not upset with me that we left everyone behind?"

The gelding snorted, ears flicking back and then forward as he kept walking. They'd been riding at a slow but steady pace, stopping only when the light became too faint to see, and rising to begin again once light reappeared, less out of any sense of urgency than the fact that Gabriel had no reason to linger in any one place.

His sense of the Road had returned once they left the hollow where he'd woken, as though it had been blurred with his memories, but every sinew in his body told him to stay on the faint path that led him further into the empty desert.

And still, every time he reached to find a source of water, no matter how small, he could hear the faintest echo of Grandmother River's call. He had not gone far enough away yet.

4

It took fourteen days for the echo to fade entirely. On the fifteenth day, Gabriel found himself, having made camp, staring up at the sky with no inclination to move. The moon was waxing again, casting the stars into its shadow. He was reminded of a story he'd heard once, although he could not remember from what tribe, that said the stars were shards of the moon's brightness, and they were afraid of being gathered within his embrace once again and so only came out most clearly when he was at his weakest.

He knew that wasn't true. Back in the States he'd listened to lecturers argue about the birthing of planets in terms of science, not magic, but there was a comfort in thinking that the stars were in the same predicament he was, and yet managed to endure.

He also suspected that he was running a fever, to be thinking such things.

"You can all take a... a long leap off a high cliff," he told the stars, or maybe it was the moon-silvered wren that was sitting on a charred, prickly stump by the smoldering fire, staring at him when it should still have been sleeping. "I've not left the

Territory"—though he was skirting painfully close to the border, if his sense of where they were could still be trusted —"and I'm not spouting any wounds to get infected, so there's no reason for me to be ill, at all."

The last time he'd fallen sick, it had been after the ghost-cat had raked him with her claws. Isobel had been there to make camp for them and scold him until he rested. It had been nice, after so long traveling alone, to have someone to care for him. Someone else to care for.

He frowned, rubbing at his too-flushed face. Who would do that for her now, if she fell ill? Auntie, maybe. Or the marshal and his daughter. But when she left Red Stick, when she once again traveled the Dust Roads, doing the devil's work? Isobel was too easily caught up in her duties, too certain it all rested on her...

"You're really worrying about her instead of yourself?"

He turned his head, somehow unsurprised to see the great shaggy bulk sitting cross-legged next to him, although the rational part of his thoughts knew that Graciendo was weeks distant even by fast horse, tucked away in his mountain isolation.

His mouth felt too dry to move, but he managed a half-smile. "Hello, Old Bear."

The salutation did not soften the other's growl. "It would serve you right if you died out here, of sheer foolishness. Did you learn nothing from what I taught you?"

"Um." His tongue felt thick and slow; his throat dry as sand. "You told me to stay away from people, and," and he tried to wave an arm at the emptiness around them, but his elbow wouldn't lift, "here I am."

Graciendo growled at him. "I told you to keep your distance from civilization, to stay free of entanglements, not to dig yourself a hole and die in it. Although I see you've shed yourself of the devil's tool."

"Her name's Isabel," and he had trouble shaping her name, the es sound turning into a zee. "And I didn't mean to leave her. It just... happened."

The River had wiped her from his thoughts, and he still didn't understand why.

"Hrmph." The old bear's paw rested lightly on his forehead, the pinprick of massive black claws only a suggestion against his skin. "Foolish boy. Always foolish. You need water."

He didn't *want* water. That was the point. Gabriel tried to sneer, but his lips were suddenly too dry and cracked to draw back, and he wondered when that had happened. How long had they been talking? How long had he been here?

His gaze flicked upward, trying to find the moon again, but the sky was too filled with stars now, a dizzying splay glittering like water over rocks, ice draped from bare tree branches, and somewhere in there, eyes peered down at him, blinking golden-yellow.

"I warned you about this. You never listen."

"Blah, blah blah." Gabriel's tongue felt thick, and hard to move in his mouth.

One of Graciendo's paws moved down the side of his face, the tip of the smallest claw dipping into Gabriel's mouth, pulling the lower lip down. The faintest wet drop touched his flesh, and he tasted salt and iron. A reminder that Graciendo, for all that he'd chosen to care for Gabriel in his own way, was still creature of the Territory; as dangerous as any magician and twice as unpredictable for never having been human even to start.

"Don't," he said, trying to spit it out. He'd no idea what that blood might do to him, no desire to find out.

The claw dug deeper, another drop hitting his tongue.

"Not even wolves can live on dry bones," Graciendo said. "What were you thinking, riding into the driest of dry lands? That's no place for you."

Gabriel had no logical answer, so he only glared.

There was a pause, then a heavy sigh, musty and fish-scented, gusted across his skin. "Dying's no terrible thing, but dying stupid?"

The bloody moisture was enough to make his tongue work again. "Not gonna die."

"Yes, you will. But not today."

The claw shifted away from his mouth, but the paw remained, the rough leather of his palm cool against Gabriel's cheek. Not a threat, not a promise, simply a touch. Graciendo might grumble and fuss, but he would not force anything on him. Not even force him to live.

Gabriel had first stumbled into the seemingly-abandoned cabin on the flanks of the Mother's Knife, young, stupid, and half-mad, still running from Old Woman Who Never Dies and her words of warning, her sealing his fate.

The shifter was old. Older than the devil even, Gabriel suspected, and even now, decades later, Gabriel still did not know why the shifter had taken him in rather than rending him limb from limb. But he had, giving him space and –time—and advice—until Gabriel came back to his senses.

If you don't let it take you, it can't have you, Old Bear had said. *It can't do anything without your say-so. Keep saying no and mean it, and the Territory can't claim you.*

Gabriel, young, foolish, and half-mad, had thought that would be simple.

"He said I'd be done. When I was done." Even in his own thoughts that hadn't made much sense, but Graciendo just nodded, coarse black hair falling in disarray over his face before being swiped back with a muttered growl so familiar Gabriel felt himself smile, cracked lips be damned. The old bear had growled around him like that for weeks before speaking a single word.

"There's done, and then there's done," the shifter said now.

"You're not that boy any longer. The fear, the terror that gnawed on you then, you starved it. Beat it down. You're not healed, not whole by a far call, but closer than you were. Closer than I thought you could be. So, tell me, Gabriel. Are you ready to be done? Or do you just think you should be?"

Gabriel narrowed his eyes at the shifter. "You told me—"

"I told you what you needed to know then. Now I'm telling you what you need to know now. What you do with it, that's always been your call, no-one else's. The River's not going to do it for you."

The words made no sense, making his head buzz like a hive had set up residence inside.

"Leave me alone." Gabriel turned his head away, scowling up at the sky.

There was another deep, musty sigh, and when Gabriel turned back a second later to apologize for his churlishness, he was alone.

THE OLD BEAR may have been a hallucination, but the fever was not. Gabriel was reasonable certain the sun had risen and set any number of times since he'd made camp, but he couldn't swear to it. The landscape wavered around him, and the sky was filled with colors, and when the sweats came, he was too warm, then the chills came and he tried to get up, to find a blanket or fire, but couldn't move his body off the bedroll.

If Graciendo had left him here to die, he was well on his way to it.

At some point he knew that Steady had laid down next to him, the familiar smell of warm horse-sweat and leather almost enough to keep him from shivering, but when he woke again, the moon a bare crescent in the black-blue sky, the horse was nowhere to be found.

Panic hit him then: if something had happened to Steady, he would never forgive himself. He was struggling to untangle himself from his blanket when a faint shhhhing noise sounded near his head, and he froze.

"Relax, little coussssssssin," the snake told him, but it sounded irritated rather than amused, and an irritated snake did not make him feel reassured. "The horsssssssse isssss fine, only sssssssssleeeeping."

Riding with Isobel had made spirit animal visitations a more common if always unnerving occurrence; he did not welcome their return. He was not, however, fool enough to say so.

The snake moved forward, its body gliding across the dry dirt with only the faintest of sounds, and Gabriel tried not to react as its heavy, red-and-gold striped weight slid up onto his body, weaving its length until the bulk of it rested on his torso, the head raised so it could look down into Gabriel's face.

Snake eyes should be black, beady. These, set deep in the narrow scaled face, were the color of the moon overhead.

"You again?" Gabriel asked, although he could not have said if this was the same snake that had spoken to him before or another, or if all spirit animals were in fact the same. "You gonna scold me, too?"

"You are a fool, and the bear thrice a fool," the snake told him, in a voice that allowed for no argument, and then darted forward, its fangs visible only long enough for Gabriel to panic again before they struck, digging deep into his face, into the flesh of his cheek just below the bone.

It hurt like hell.

When Gabriel woke again, the sky overhead was thick with dark blue clouds, Steady was grazing peacefully a few feet from his head, and he was covered in a thick blanket woven in a bright red and yellow pattern he did not recognize. The fever seemed to have broken overnight. He moved his arm—and he was pleased to see that it raised without protest—sliding out from under the blanket to touch his cheek, testing the warmth of his skin. Sweaty, but cool. He pressed with his fingers and winced at the unexpected twinge of soreness. He remembered...

Snake.

He sat upright, the blanket falling off him, and pressed his hand again against the skin where the dream-snake had bitten him, uncertain as to why the flesh there was not torn open, why he was not dead, the flesh of his cheek not filled with venom, but rather plumped with water.

Graciendo had left him to choose death, but the snake...

The snake had taken that choice from him. Once again, the Territory moved him, manipulated him like a chess piece. Worse, like a chess piece without a board, played for some purpose he could not understand.

What reason was there in keeping him alive? He had served his purpose for Isobel; the spirit world should have no further need of him.

He plucked at the blanket, frowning at the unfamiliar weave of browns and greens. It wasn't his. He would have woken had anyone come within the circle of salt, and Steady certainly would have alerted him if anyone had come close enough to drape a blanket over him; the horse was as good as a sentry in that regard.

And yet.

He looked around nonetheless, and then looked up, and up again, into the branches of a tree that had not been there when he'd laid down the night before.

Now full-awake, he blinked, barely daring to breathe. But not even closing his eyes and pinching the back of his hand made the vision disappear.

It was without doubt a tree, growing at the foot of his bedroll and reaching ten feet or more into the sky, limbs bare and trunk smooth-green and entirely impossible, because it had not been there the night—days? before.

It was not the strangest thing Gabriel had seen, but not even the past few years could make him think it ordinary.

Gabriel looked around again more carefully, noting the intact salt circle, the angled rock he'd placed his boots on before crawling into his bedroll, the line of slow-greening tumbleweed and clusters of sunwork flowers he'd noted when making camp. Nothing had moved, nothing had changed. Nothing save that there was now a tree where there had been none before.

"Well then." When faced with unknown medicine of an unknown source, a wise Rider was above all polite. "Hello."

The tree did not respond. Gabriel almost felt hurt.

In addition to the tree, and the blanket he did not recognize, there was a pack resting against the trunk that also had not been there before. He crawled forward enough to grab it by a strap, bringing it closer with caution, as though the tree might bend down to catch at him with those long bare limbs. But nothing stirred, nothing sprung out to attack, nor did the tree, as he'd half-feared, shift shape into anything else.

Whatever games the Territory was playing on him, it did not seem to be a violent one.

The brown leather of the pack was cracked and worn, but the seams looked to be water-tight, and under the buckled flap were a sack bag of dried beans, another of dried corn, and a cloth bag of tortillas, then another smaller bag of what smelled like a medicinal tea, and a battered tin plate on top of a leather canteen that, when unstoppered, proved to be filled with fresh, cool water. No meat, but he supposed that was too much to ask of his benefactors.

He had told the old bear that he was not going to die. It appeared that the Territory was determined to keep him from becoming a liar.

What he did with it, Graciendo had said, was up to him.

"My thanks, Cousin Snake," he said out loud, and replaced the stopper in the canteen. "And you too, Old Bear, if this is any of your doing." It seemed unlikely—the shifter to have called for such a thing, and the spirit-snake to heed him—but the other choice, that a spirit-snake was keeping close-enough watch on him, that a spirit-snake cared enough to watch him, was twice as unnerving and Gabriel wanted no part of it. He did not want to be important. He wanted to be left alone.

Did he want to be done?

Desperately. Desperately, he wanted to be done. But not today.

Replacing everything into the pack, he sat up, crosslegged, and again considered the tree in front of him. Without leaves he could not easily identify it, but the shape seemed familiar somehow. He let his knowledge of the Territory's plant life run through his memory, but nothing matched. Standing up, he walked, unsteadily, over to it. His fingers itched to touch the bark, but he kept his hands shoved into his pockets and merely looked. From a distance it had looked smooth-trunked, but up close, even under the dim daylight, he could see where there were striations along the surface, bits of thin bark peeling away, as though the tree were shedding its skin like a snake.

Snakes again.

He shook his head and looked up at the branches reaching into the sky, their tips forming an almost perfect arc.

His breath caught as he realized where he had seen that silhouette before, time and again: in the sigil of the Road Marshals. The world-tree, the joining of bone and wind, constrained within the silver loop.

"Jordan wash me clean." He had traveled with the Devil's Hand, had seen the brand on her palm glow with power, had seen... had seen more than most liars would dare to claim. He should not have been capable of awe any more.

And yet. And yet.

"It's just a tree," he said out loud, and the dryness in his throat made him back up, reaching for the canteen. The first sip made him want to gulp more, but he forced himself to take it slow, letting a single mouthful roll around in his mouth before letting himself swallow, feeling his throat constrict around the wetness as though reluctant to let go. The fever still rested in him, although lessened enough that he could think without the weight of a fog, and after four careful swallows, he poured a small amount into his cupped hands.

"Hey, boy," he called to the gelding. "No creek nearby, I'm sorry."

Steady's head lifted and his nostrils flared, clearly catching the scent of fresh water. He walked over and lowered his head to the offering, ruffling softly at it before taking the water up, spilling a little onto the blanket as he did so.

"Easy there," Gabriel said, reaching up to stroke the muscular neck with a damp hand. "More where that came, from, but not so much we can be foolish."

The horse's hide was cool and smooth, with no sign of having been neglected or thirsty. He suspected, if he looked carefully, he would find tiny fang marks somewhere on the horse's legs, too.

"Thank you," Gabriel said out loud. "For this, and for all else you have done."

He had no idea what the tree growing out of nowhere meant, what lesson he was supposed to take from its sudden appearance, if there was in fact any lesson at all. But he had been fool enough to ride into the desert without supplies; he would not worsen his foolishness by being disrespectful of the gift, no matter what price he would, eventually, inevitably, pay for it.

And he would pay, he knew that. He had thrown the

gauntlet into the Mudwater, and he'd thought she'd thrown it back. But now...

What he did with it was up to him.

He looked around at the desolate campsite, down at the blanket and pack, then up again at the tree, the rising sunlight shimmering around the branches.

"Whatever your purpose," he told it, "I want no part. Do you understand?"

Despite a reasonable certainty that the tree would do him no harm, Gabriel had wanted to pack up and ride out immediately, to get as far from its unnerving appearance as possible, but the simple act of walking around the campfire had made his legs quiver with exhaustion and sweat break out on his skin. There was no way he'd be able to stay in the saddle for any length of time, even at a walk.

"Looks like we're here for a bit," he told Steady, who had moved cautiously closer to the tree, cropping at the dry grass with vague interest. "And you." Gabriel looked up at the tree, telling himself the tree was *not* looking back at him. "Don't... do anything."

He told himself that he only imagined the sound of slithering laughter, rising from the grass.

It took two more days for the fever to wear off and his strength to come back. Gabriel dozed and woke, eating a little each time, sipping from the canteen enough to keep his mouth wet and his urine regular, staggering away from the messy nest he'd made of his bedroll to relieve himself and then staggering back, checking on Steady each time. The horse drank the rest and, somehow, the canteen never quite ran dry. Gabriel was careful not to question it.

Graciendo was there occasionally, sometimes human, often

not. Gabriel was reasonably certain it was a fever-dream, but it might not have been.

"I should have killed you," Old Bear said one night, casually, holding his scarred hands out over the fire as though to warm them.

"Probably." He might even have been looking to die at that point; the memory of it, like so much of that year, was hazed to Gabriel still.

"Do you know why I did not?"

"Amusement."

The expected growl of laughter did not come. "Because the end comes soon enough, and it comes for us all. Even me, some day. Even the devil, curse his faces. I've brought the end to many who asked for it, and more who did not, and never regretted it. But it has never not been a waste."

The heavy head swung to look at him, eyes flickering red in the firelight, and despite himself, Gabriel shivered.

"When your end comes, let it not be a waste."

WHEN GABRIEL WOKE the next morning, Graciendo was gone, but another shape sat at his fire. Human, female, and for a moment his memory failed him again. "Izzy?"

But when she turned, it was a stranger.

"You've been careless," the woman said with a smirk. "You forgot to ward your fire."

"No." He had, he knew that, remembered clearly one of the last things he'd done the very first night, dragging himself out of the bedroll to spread salt in a wide circle around the small camp. He remembered the feel of the grains sticking to his sweat-slicked hand, the taste of it bitter-sharp on his tongue.

It was possible, in his fever, he'd broken it somehow, but

Graciendo would not have left him unprotected. Not without warning.

He thought of the last conversation they'd had and wondered if that had been the warning. But why?

The woman shrugged as though his denial was of no matter to her. "Figured you wouldn't mind if I borrowed your fire for a bit." There was the smell of coffee, sharp and bitter, in the air; she'd been there a while, while he slept.

He managed to sit up, the blanket falling into his lap, and noted that her knife lay on a rock by her knee, within easy reach, and a bow, unstrung, and quiver rested behind her. There was no sign of a firearm, but from the easy assurance with which she knelt at his fire, comfortable turning her back to him, he suspected she would not need one to be dangerous.

Despite her attire, she wasn't a Rider; no Rider would use another's fire without first gaining permission, no matter how feverish he might have been. She wasn't native either, from the look of her; dark hair curling in wisps around her ears and neck, visible skin rose-tinted and slightly burnt from the sun.

"You going to rob me?"

"You have anything worth taking?"

"Not particularly, no."

"Then I'll just use your fire and be on my way," she said.

Gabriel considered his options, found them limited, and lay back down again, pulling the blanket back over his shoulder. "Wake me before you go," he said, and closed his eyes again, the tree a reassuring shadow over him.

He did not quite sleep but dozed peacefully and without dreams until he felt the harp sting of pebbles glancing off his body. He started, his hand reaching for his blade even as he struggled to his feet.

"Whoa, whoa." She held up her hands, dropping the remaining pebbles back to the ground. "Easy there, Rider. I'm on my way now."

Despite her earlier words, he cast a glance at his pack, still leaning against the tree, but it looked undisturbed.

"I told you I wouldn't." She sounded almost hurt that he'd doubted her.

"You're a bandit," he said. "I'd be a fool to assume you didn't at least look."

She grinned at that, and her face went sharp as a fox. "Oh, I did. You were right, you've nothing particularly worth stealing. Except maybe your horse, but I thought trying that might not be worth the blood."

Steady would not have gone gently, she was right in that.

He glanced at the sky, gauging from the sun's light that it was just past mid-day. He tested his body, felt a lingering dizziness that told him likely should sit down again before he fell. He shifted closer to the fire and folded his legs under him in what he hoped was a graceful collapse.

"Where are you going?"

"Why do you care?"

He shrugged, sliding his knife out of its sheath at his thigh and using the tip of it to poke at the fire. She'd banked it, but warmth still rose from the glowing embers. "Always good to know what's up ahead." Bandits rarely ran alone; if she was heading to a nearby camp, he wanted to make sure to go the other direction.

"Even less ahead than there was behind. Not even the Tua spend time out here they don't have to. Too many ghosts."

Tua. He was in Tua lands. Gabriel filed that information in a corner of his mind before flicking a quick look around, as though expecting the uneasy dead to appear at the fire. "Haints?"

She pursed her lips, eyes narrowing. "Ghosts, haunts, spirits of the dead, it's all much the same, innit?"

No. It decidedly wasn't. And much depended on *whose* ghosts they were. But he'd no desire to argue with a bandit, however polite she'd been so far. Instead he gave her a tight, bright smile, showing all of his teeth. "Then I'll be sure not to linger, thank you."

He waited until the bandit had gone on her way and then waited a little while longer, knife resting at his knee until he was reasonably certain she had not brought friends back around with her. He occasionally checked the silver set into his knife and belt buckle for tarnish, but there was no indication of the metal blackening any since he'd last polished them, the visible sign that power was gathering around him.

That did not mean something did not lurk just beyond notice, however. Magicians and whatnot, the pooling of power at a crossroads? Silver could be trusted on those things. The lurking of things *of* power, such as spirit animals or haints? Less certain, he'd learned that the hard way.

And if Graciendo had been keeping them at bay, that protection had clearly ended.

Gabriel glanced up at the tree again, wondering if it was the reason he remained unmolested. Better not to trust it. Better not to trust anything save himself.

Reaching over, he pulled his pack to him and removed the small leather sack of coins, pouring them out on a nearby flat rock. Hilts and buckles were well and fine, but coins were of purer stuff. If anything stronger than a dust-devil stirred nearby, he'd know.

Reassured, he moved to the fire to start his own breakfast. The bandit had finished her coffee, but left a pan—his own pan, he noted with dry amusement—to the side of the fire, bits of cooked meat resting in it.

"I'd be a poor host, to refuse a guest-price," he told Steady, who had wandered a little closer now that the stranger was gone, dropping his head and twitching his tail in what passed for an equine slouch. Gabriel ate the meal, and let the fire die down, placing the new coalstone into the stone circle instead and pressing down on it just enough to bring up a gentle warmth as the afternoon faded away.

Every now and again he stirred the handful of silver, checking for tarnish.

He should be moving on. Even if she had been lying about this place being haunted, even if the tree was protecting him, there was no source of fresh water once the canteen ran out, and little grazing for Steady. His earlier dizziness was nearly gone. One more night, and then they would ride.

"If there are haints here," he said, stirring the coins again with one finger, "you should know I've seen worse than you before, and not blinked."

A haint was restless, but not vicious, not without cause. And he'd had no cause in any deaths here, nor had he killed anything recently. They'd no reason to attack him.

Ghosts, on the other hand... you could never tell with ghosts.

He turned to look at the tree, rising up against the afternoon sky, reddish winter sunlight shining through its bare branches. A spirit-snake, and a world-tree. When he'd ridden with the Devil's Hand, he might have expected some such thing to happen on any given third day. Isobel had reached deeper into the bones than he'd thought possible, become as much one with the Territory as human flesh could, and not lose her way. The tree would have made sense, had she been there.

Nothing makes sense. Another memory: Graciendo sitting crosslegged on his cot, in the cottage half-hidden in the high foothills of the Mother's Knife. *You tell yourself it does, you look for patterns and make up stories. But there's no sense to it at all.*

After the well-meant brutality of Old Woman Who Never Dies, Graciendo's almost nonchalant words had been soothing, calming. But in the years since, he'd come to realize that taking life advice from a being as old as Graciendo likely was had its own flaws. "Keep your distance from civilization." Graciendo had said that, more than once. Had told him that the only way to stay clear of the Territory's snares was to be as small and insignificant on its flanks as a fly, neither biting nor stinging.

And it had worked, until Gabriel had been fool enough to ride into Flood, and offer his hand to a young girl with an interesting face.

Graciendo had not wanted anything to do with Isobel, had refused them shelter, when Gabriel brought them 'round. Admittedly, the presence of the magician Farron Easterly had influenced that, but the curl of Old Bear's lip had been for Isobel herself—or, more accurately, for her master.

Graciendo said he'd healed, but all Gabriel could feel was a yawning, aching emptiness. Not worse than what had driven him before, but he was no longer half-mad. Or perhaps he was all mad, now. That would explain much.

"What would Isobel do," Gabriel wondered out loud, surprised at how rough and crackling his voice sounded.

Isobel would pack up the gifts given to her, and ride on.

Ride where, was the question. Where, and to what?

He couldn't go back.

He looked back at the tree, watching as the sunlight cast a shadow from it, like a grotesquely elongated sun dial. Driven by some resonant instinct, he reached for the sensation of water below ground, thinking to trace them to the tree's root, get some sense of it that way. But he'd no sooner begun than he stopped with an almost physical jolt, dry nausea surging in his throat, every gut nerve he owned snapping like dry wood in a storm.

If he touched the tree, it would find him.

His body recoiled in reaction, and he dropped to his knees, panting heavily. "Mother of a backward mule!"

His left hand reached for his knife, fingers of his right hand twitching in tradesign gestures he'd not used since he was a child, to deter malign intent.

For a moment, just a moment, he was that boy again, half-drowned and terrified, broken and alone, starting at every touch of power, hiding from the medicine in his own bones.

Slowly, he unclenched his fingers, pulled his hand away from the knife. His breathing slowed, although his heart still beat too quickly for comfort, and his skin was soaked in cold, stinking sweat.

The tree did not move, the branches still, the faint budding knobs a pale, unassuming green.

There was no reason to be afraid. For years, the River had left him alone, had waited until he came close enough to reach out again, and now he was far away, and riding further. The echoes of the Mudwater had faded. The most he might find here would be smaller tributaries, ones that had no awareness of him, no awareness of anything save themselves. There *should* be no threat, at least. But Gabriel had learned to trust his instincts, had learned to protect himself.

The River would ignore him? Then he would ignore it, as well. It, and the devil, and Graciendo, too, if the old bear wasn't going to be useful.

"Not as though folk don't muddle along perfectly well without the Touch," he told Steady, laying the gift—blanket on top of his bedroll and packing it up into its usual place on the saddle. "I've gotten lazy, relying on it."

The horse snorted at him, unimpressed.

HE SLEPT DEEPLY, with no dreams, and the next morning, as he'd expected, he felt confident in riding on.

It took Gabriel a moment to determine the best way to add the new pack, which lacked the familiar straps, to the saddle as well, but he was able to rig it using a spare lash of leather to make sure it hung securely. Hopefully not even Steady's ground-eating gallop would dislodge it, and hopefully they would have no need of galloping.

The beast in question, unused to a rider who fumbled so much with their gear, craned its neck to watch what he was doing. Gabriel kept one eye on the whiskered muzzle and square, blunt teeth. Unlike the mule, Steady was not prone to nipping at unprotected backsides, but Gabriel knew better than to assume, or to think that his horse did not have a sense of humor that occasionally showed itself in painful ways.

"There. All set and tidy."

After gathering up the coins and dropping them into his pocket, he settled his hat firmly on his head and took another moment to survey the campsite. The tree, standing tall in the midst of the drylands, would doubtless draw the attention of any travelers to follow, so he left the stones of the fire circle as they were rather than breaking it down. For the rest, only the piled-over hole where he'd relieved himself and the flattened earth where his bedroll had been, remained as evidence that anyone had been there, much less lingered for several days.

If this place was haunted, as the bandit had claimed, the haints did not seem to have minded his presence. But still, it would only be good caution to acknowledge his unintended guest-debt.

Reaching into his pocket, his fingers found the smoothed-over edges of a quarter-coin and pulled it out. Placing it back on the smoothed stone, he made the tradesign for 'thank you,' and then 'let us be done.'

The wind remained calm, the ground still, no indication that anything within miles was paying attention. With a shrug, Gabriel swung up into the saddle, pausing a moment to allow a faint dizziness to pass. Years of habit and training made him press down into the saddle, leg tightening around Steady's bulk, even as he settled himself into the stirrups.

His stomach was tight against his spine, his bladder empty

as the landscape, and the remnants of the fever yet drifted around his ears, but he still felt better on horseback than he had sitting on the ground.

And then there was no more reason to delay. He scanned the area around him and then with a shrug, laid the reins against Steady's neck, put the sun to his forehead, and headed west again.

PASSIM

Before Man shaped mud in his own image, before any creatures burrowed, crawled, or flew, before demon or spirit struck mischief in the world, there was bone, and there was wind, and there was water. And they did not speak to one another, for what purpose was there in that?

That is where the story began. In the not-speaking, in the not-touching. In the emptiness between.

That is where the story always begins. When the pieces touch, and the speaking begins.

5

Gabriel had forgotten how annoying demons were. Annoying, irritating, obnoxious, plaguey.... He was running out of words to describe it, but the demon kept *talking*.

"Worthless, useless human. Bits of bone and piss, dusty dust drifting down into the road to be ridden on, peed on, forgotten."

The demon had shown up a few hours after he'd broken camp and ridden out, appearing and then disappearing again like a ghost-cat stalking it prey, its dark-mottled skin blending nearly perfectly with the rocks and cacti every time Gabriel tried to get a clear glimpse of it, only the swirl of colors when it moved giving it away. The chanting had only started an hour or so back, but already, Gabriel was heartily tired of it.

"Better dust than a madcake of mud like you," he shot back, then cursed himself again for even acknowledging the thing. Demon were annoyances, problematic creatures more intelligent than they seemed, but less a threat to the wary traveler than they wished. That was not to say that they weren't dangerous, but a little caution cut the risk significantly. There might be others, waiting for Gabriel to be caught distracted, but he doubted it. Demons rarely clumped together, more likely to attack each other than to conspire. And this one seemed determined to announce its presence every step of the way, eliminating any possible sneak attack.

Unless it meant to kill him through sheer vexation, always a possibility.

"Pisswater and bone-meal. These roads are ground from the bones of your kind," the demon sneered, finally varying its chant. Gabriel rolled his eyes, using the kerchief looped around his neck to wipe sweat off his face.

"Yeah, that's why we call 'em the Dust Roads," he said in return, injecting just the right amount of bored lecturer into his tone. The nickname had come from Riders originally, a wry acknowledgment of their eventual fate; did the demon think its words were somehow startling or discouraging?

"I should have gone toward the bandit's camp," he muttered, shoving a hand through his sweat-sticky hair before replacing his hat. "At least they'd have whisky to go with the taunting."

"Didn't you used to ride double?" The demon appeared ahead of him this time, stepping out from behind a crossway cactus. Its face was flat as a pebble, its mouth clay-red and leering. "Pretty little thing. Oh, and the Hand, too."

Gabriel felt the temptation to load the carbine with rock salt and see how the demon enjoyed that but cleaning the barrel of residue afterward probably wasn't worth it.

"I'll be sure to pass along the compliment to Flatfoot. Gotta warn you, though, the mule'd be more likely to stomp you into goo than play nice." He grinned at the thought, and it wasn't a nice grin. "And if you were thinking in the other direction, the Hand would scrape you up on her toast."

The demon made a kissy noise and disappeared again behind a rock. Gabriel didn't quite hold his breath, but when Steady had gone several strides further and the air around them remained silent, he may have exhaled a little in relief. If he'd known invoking Isobel would make the demon scamper, he would have done it hours ago.

"Still and all," he said out loud when he felt he might not be jinxing himself, "if something felt the need to harass us, better demon than magician."

Steady's ears flicked back and forth as though in agreement. The horses hadn't liked Farron Easterly much either, Gabriel recalled, although the mule had been quickly won over. Sometimes Gabriel wondered about Flatfoot, he truly did. Then again, the mule had adored Isobel from the start as well.

"Cozying up to the uncanny, should expect nothing else from a mule," he said, taking off his hat to wipe the sweat from his forehead yet again.

Too much time in the mountains, and then down south; he'd forgotten how warm the desert could become, even in winter. They'd been riding steadily since dawn, the sun keeping pace with them overhead, and a wiser man would have made camp come noon, waiting until the afternoon shadows to move on. And yet Gabriel could not bring himself to stop, feeling as though the world-tree was still just at his back, outstretched branches looming over him. The first few times he'd twisted in the saddle to look; now he clamped down on the urge, grit his teeth, and kept looking ahead.

Not that there was much to see. The trail they were following cut through rolling hills, the higher ridge of a mountain running to their right, tips still blanketed with the grey-white of snow, but the land around him was a green and gray winterscape of grass and stone. The bandit hadn't exaggerated; this was a barren place. Even the animal life was scarce, the occasional rustle of something in the grass or a bird swooping low overhead the only signs of life before the demon had shown up.

He didn't miss the demon at all but suspected that might

change if the scenery didn't become more interesting soon. He'd lost the knack of riding alone.

"Think she's all right?" He didn't wait for an ear-flick this time, but went on, "Yeah, she's all right." He took comfort in the earlier reassurance but did not try to reach out again; when you were given an unexpected gift, it was better not to return to that well uninvited. Some things took offense at that.

He tilted his head back, pushing his hat back enough to squint up at the sky. Ink-dark clouds were beginning to form along the horizon, obscuring the edge of the mountains and stretching into the direction they were heading. "Rain tonight. Better hope we find a decent campsite, or we're in for a soggy supper."

HE MISJUDGED; the first drop began to fall well before nightfall, thick, heavy drops that found their way down the back of his collar and worked their way up his pants' leg, turning the sandy soil underfoot into a slick mess. Steady lived up to his name, each heavy hoof coming down with deliberate precision, but his head hung low and his flanks shuddered occasionally, indicating his displeasure. They were both Road-hardened, but this sort of cold, wind-driven rain was nothing man nor beast should be out in.

In the mountains there would have been rock overhangs to shelter under, and in the woods he'd have bent branches into protection, but there was no help for it here but to keep moving. Camping now was out of the question: the soil could only hold so much water before it would refuse it, throwing up fierce torrents that could wash a man's camp away before he'd woken and drown him in the process.

It might be suitably ironic for water to kill him that way, but Gabriel had no desire for that to be his epitaph.

At least the sense of the world-tree, like the Mudwater, had finally faded into the distance, or perhaps been washed away by the rain.

By the time the clouds darkened enough for him to determine the sun had set, Gabriel would have welcomed the demon's return, if only for there to be something other than the weight of sodden cloth and the endless tickle of a sneeze building in the back of his throat to distract him. He might well have bargained his soul for a crackling fire and a cup of warm *anything*. But the landscape, other than rising slightly, sandy soil turning to slippery rocks, did not change, and he resigned himself to continuing throughout the night and making camp when the sun rose or the rains stopped, whichever came first.

"What the—" Steady had halted, all four limbs gathering square under him, and Gabriel shifted out of his half-dozing state: tension sung throughout the horse's body, telling his rider that he'd sensed or seen something the human could not. "All right boy, I got ya." He gathered the reins lightly in one hand, reassuring the horse that he was paying attention now, and settled his breathing, ears straining to hear anything past the steady beat of the rain.

Just as he was deciding that whatever Steady had reacted to had moved on, there was a shift of shadows to his left, then a voice came out of the darkness, deep, male, and filled with amusement.

"If you've no desire to turn into a fish, you might want to come with us."

Gabriel had no idea who was speaking, or where they might be leading him, but his other options were even less appealing, so he turned Steady toward the source of the voice and moved him forward into a walk again.

Much to his surprise and pleasure, the shadowed voice—which turned into a shadowed figure on horseback, draped in an oilskin that Gabriel was deeply jealous of —soon led him not to an encampment, but an actual shed, complete with a door and a roof that did not leak. The floor underneath was soft, and when the rider reached up to light a lantern hanging overhead, Gabriel saw to his astonishment that it was covered not with straw or grasses, but brownish-green *rugs*, layered against each other to create a patchwork flooring.

"We're here," his companion said needlessly, sliding down from his own horse, which, Gabriel was able to see now, bore neither saddle nor bridle, just a loose rope halter. The stranger pulled the oilcloth off his body and hung it on a hook, and in doing so reminded Gabriel that he was sitting like a fool, dripping wet. He slid down, wincing as his boots squelched wetly on the rugs.

"Don't worry, they're old. Here," and the man threw him something, Gabriel caught it instinctively. It was a small towel, threadbare but dry. "Won't do you much good, but it'll be enough to wipe yourself down until we can get to a fire."

Gabriel took off his hat and mopped his face and neck dry, studying the other man as he bought his horse to the far end of the shed, where he dumped a pail of grain into a wooden trough. In the lamplight, his savior was a narrow-built man, greying hair slicked against his skull, a sharply pointed beard covering his chin, and skin the color of a well-worn saddle. He turned to look at Gabriel, then grinned, showing several missing teeth. "Looks like we got you before you went all fish-like after all. Well, make your beast comfortable, and come on."

There was a hook in the wall for the bridle, and a wooden ledge below to store the saddle. Gabriel hesitated a moment, then shrugged and left his pack and saddlebags with it. If he had in fact fallen in with bandits, they would rob him will he nill he. But there was no reason to give offense up front in *presuming* that they would.

Expecting to have to go back out into the rain, he was pleas-antly surprised that instead his guide led him through a narrow door at the other end of the shed, and out into a covered walk-way. The rain fell in sheets on either side, but the path itself remained dry, the stones crunching softly underfoot. Through the downpour, he could see other buildings in what looked like a half-circle stretching away from the shed. If this was a bandit's enclave, they were more profitable than he would have expected, this far from anywhere.

"I'm Henry, by the way," his companion said, almost as an afterthought.

"Gabriel."

"Pleasure to meet you, Gabriel. Welcome to Rabbit's Mound."

THE PATH LED to a larger structure, a low-ceilinged hall filled with long wooden tables, currently filled with nearly two dozen bodies, adults and children, plus a handful of shaggy-coated dogs lounging about on the stone floor without regard for the humans who had to step over them or risk spilling their meals. A few of the adults paused what they were doing to look at him, but most went about their conversations as though having a dripping-wet stranger appear was nothing out of the ordinary.

From the way Henry was acting, Gabriel decided, it may have been. Did they make a point of rescuing bedraggled trav-elers? Or had he merely been fortunate that Henry was out in the rain?

"Miguel!" Henry veered off to yell into an adjoining room. From the aroma and clatter coming from within, Gabriel deter-mined that it was a kitchen, even as a man appeared in the doorway, a wooden spoon in one hand and a long apron covering him from chest to feet.

"Whatever you're slopping up, make it two, please," Henry said, then looked back at the room. "And someone get us a towel and a rug! Man's dripping to death and nobody wants his haint hanging around the fire, do they?"

Before Gabriel had time to look around more, he found himself seated on a smooth wooden bench in front of the fire burning steadily inside a semi-circular stone fire pit, a narrow chimney bringing the smoke up and out through the roof. There were more rugs here, scattered under the tables, and one placed under his feet. Someone handed him a towel, as worn as the previous one but considerably larger, and stood patiently next to him until he realized they were waiting for him to remove his coat and hand it to them.

He did so, and the jacket underneath, leaving him in dry-but-thin shirtsleeves, and sodden trousers he had no plans to remove just then, no matter what dry replacements they brought him. He did, however, remove his boots and socks, placing them closer to the hearth to dry. He felt naked enough as-was, but again, no-one seemed to notice. The rug was warm under his toes, the wooden floor underneath that smooth and gleaming with wear.

Whatever this place was, they had been here for some time.

The towel was thin, but it soaked the damp from his hair and dried his feet, and by the time he set it aside, Henry had returned, holding two wooden bowls filled with what smelled like spiced lamb. Gabriel was not ashamed to admit that his mouth watered.

"Eat up," Henry advised, sitting down next to him and handing over one of the bowls, plus a tin spoon. "Miguel's cooking always goes fast. You come in on a night when Leah's in the kitchen... not so much."

"I heard that!" a woman's voice called for a nearby table, and Henry flipped a hand dismissively at her. "You hear me, but you're not gainsaying me, are you?"

"You take turns cooking?" The stew was, in fact, delicious, with a hint of fruity sweetness to it that he couldn't place.

"Take turn doing pretty much everything," Henry said. "Some folk got skills that can't be shared out, of course, but for the most part, yeah. That's how we survive. The Mound got started when a wagon train broke down on the way elsewhere, some thirty years back. Rest of the group went on, but some folk decided they'd rather stay put. Place suited 'em."

"You?" It was beyond rude to ask, but Henry just chuckled, tucking into his own meal. "Nah. I may look old but I ain't *that* old. My folks had a steading north of here, part of the Tua tribe lands, but I was never much of a farmer. When they died, we let the land go back to the tribe, and I ended up here. Most of us here now, we wandered in after." He nodded toward the kitchen. "Miguel came from the mountains, one of the mining towns, lost part of his leg in a cave-in. Anna and her brood came after her man died. She's a tanner, we hadn't had one of them before, so we took her in with open arms." He grinned again, the wrinkles of his face falling into position so easily Gabriel decided he probably did that a lot. "We make her work outside town proper, though. Don't know what witchcraft she uses, but it smells like things that died twice over in a heat storm."

"Tanneries tend to, yes." Gabriel's impression of the town, already positive, took another tip upward. They might not fish for travelers, but they were clearly welcoming of them. "And it looks like you've a weaver here, too?" He glanced at the nearest rug, then back at Henry.

"Mmm. The Sperrings. Entire family, for generations." He took another bite of his own stew and swallowed. "We graze sheep and goats—the bastards seem to thrive on cactus and weeds—and they turn the shearings into rugs. Traders take them for sale, all the way to Liberdad."

Liberdad was the Free Town, just south of Red Stick, where no nation claimed jurisdiction. If the rugs made it down there, they might easily be gracing homes in the States or Spain, or even France. Gabriel was impressed and thought that might explain the size of the town, and its apparent wealth.

"Do you have much tillable land?" He didn't know much about farming, but the last he'd been able to see around him, he wouldn't have thought much would grow, worth the effort it took.

Henry made a back-and-forth gesture with his hand, and a pursed lip, before saying, "Enough. We've the fortune to rest in the bend of a creek, Rabbit's Kick. Legend is that Rabbit shat here so many times on his way elsewhere, seeds sprouted and grew. That's where the town's name came from."

Henry shrugged, putting his now-empty bowl and spoon on the floor under the bench. "It's not much, but we grow and we hunt, and we make do. There's some silver that runs through the creek, Miguel taught folk how to scoop for that, and a road-trader comes through every year or so and takes up whatever we've to spare. It's makeshift and chancy, but it's home."

Gabriel looked around, noting the number of children in the room, wondering if this was the total population of the town, or if others took their meals elsewhere. "And you bring strangers into it without a thought as to the risks?"

Henry snorted. "You're one man, surrounded by dozens. That knife at your side might be sharp, but I misdoubt it could take us all, all at once?"

"I might have been a magician..."

"A magician would not have accepted the offer of aid."

Gabriel allowed, with a sideways tilt of his head, as that was likely true. Magicians were not only mad they were arrogant in their madness.

"Still. You should not be so trusting. I might be bearing a sickness."

"Then all the more reason to bring you here. We have an excellent healer, and even a priest if you feel the need to be shriven."

That raised Gabriel's eyebrows. Preachermen were not uncommon in the Territory, jumping from town to town for their keep, but a priest was far rarer. Something about close proximity to the devil made them uneasy, did not encourage them to build their churches here, although to the best of Gabriel's recollection the devil himself had never objected to their presence as such.

"I've told you before, Henry, I was not a priest, merely a brother of contemplation."

Gabriel had an excellent memory for voices. And he knew that one.

The newcomer had come up from the right side, stopping just shy of in front of them so as not to block the warmth of the fire. Stocky-built, his appearance was not particularly bettered by the brown robe he wore, but Gabriel's eye slid past that to the round, sallow-skinned face, and the close-cropped hair that emphasized surprisingly delicate ears. The last time he'd seen the man, the pate of his skull had been visible, the hair a shaggy ring around it.

"Welcome to Rabbit's Mound," the monk said, offering a hand to shake.

Gabriel set aside his bowl to take it, giving a firm grip. "Thank you.... Zacarías, yes?"

The monk's jaw dropped, and Gabriel waited, amused, as recognition stirred behind his eyes. "The—"

"Gabriel," he said overriding whatever the monk had been about to say. "Gabriel, yes."

There was no reason for him to deny his connection to Isobel, if that was what the monk had been reaching for, but there had been a simple enjoyment to being nothing more than Gabriel for the moment, and he was not quite ready to give that up.

"Gabriel. Yes."

Henry had leaned back slightly, his gaze rising to Zacarías

and then dropping back to Gabriel. "So... I have no need to introduce you, then."

"I met Gabriel on my travels before coming to the Mound," Zacarías agreed, looking far more placid than he had the last time Gabriel had seen him, in the aftermath of their battle with the spell-creature nearly a year before. A spell-creature caused by magic the Spanish King had sent across the Knife, in an attempt to undermine and unnerve the Territory. It had backfired badly, but not before several monks had died, and Gabriel had taken some nasty scars.

Gabriel mapped the Territory in his head from where he'd last seen the monk and his kin, frowning at the results. "I had thought you planned to return home?" Home across the Mother's Knife to Spanish-held lands, and not lingering in the Territory.

"God had other plans for me," the monk said with a shrug. "My brothers continued on without me, if you were thinking to ask. Only I felt the call to remain."

"He's one of ours," Henry said, the warning quiet but clear. A Spaniard in the Territory was not unheard of—travel across the Knife was difficult, but determined settlers came through nonetheless—but there were tensions nonetheless, due to that nation's overt hostility, and stated intent of expanding their borders northward.

"I've no offense with Zacarías," Gabriel assured his host. "If he felt the... call to remain, then he's as welcome as any here." That was the base of the Devil's Agreement, after all, to allow those who needed the Territory to find it, while keeping out those who saw it only as a thing to be conquered.

Gabriel might have growing doubts as how much longer the Agreement might hold against outside forces, particularly with America no longer at war and looking to expand westward as well as Spain's ambitions, but the *intent* had never been in question. If the monk abided by the Agreement, he was welcome.

The monk patted Henry's shoulder, but kept his attention on Gabriel, briefly glancing past him, and then back again. "You travel alone now?"

Gabriel licked at his lips, his toes curling in uncomfortable reflex, suddenly feeling oddly exposed. "Yes. You preach to the infidels, now?"

"I do not preach to them, no." Zacarías took the question as an invitation to join them, which Gabriel supposed in a way it had been. Pulling a wooden stool away from one of the tables, the monk sat down, looking far more comfortable on the three-legged perch than a grown man should. "I listen, when an ear is needed. I remind them of God's love."

"Occasionally he preaches," someone from the table he'd taken the stool from said, and his companions there laughed, while Henry hid a smile behind one hand and even Zacarías huffed in amusement. Whatever hesitations Gabriel had about the monk remaining in the Territory, the people here were clearly fond of him.

"Occasionally, yes, I may speak of la Sagrada Escritura. But they allow me my idiosincraias. My, ah...particularities?"

"We all have our own peculiarness," Henry agreed. "But you wield a hoe as well as anyone else, and keep us company while we guard the well, so we'll keep you for as long as you choose to stay."

Gabriel's attention was caught by part of that sentence. "Guard the well?"

Both men lost their amused expressions at that, and Zacarías gave another shrug, this one not quite as nonchalant, bending his no-longer-tonsured head toward Henry as though to cede the explanation to him.

"Despite your experiences today, we're not exactly in the land of free-flowing water, once winter's rainy season ends."

Gabriel grunted agreement at the understatement, and Henry's mouth quirked in a half-smile.

"So, the story goes that the ones who came first to Rabbit's Kick, Old John and his kin, they nearly died one summer when the land went dry and hot and the creek disappeared. They made it through with the help of some of the Tua, the local tribe they'd come to Agreement with, but Old John wasn't one to be beholden to another soul if he could avoid it. He called in all his kin and put them to work digging a well deep into the bones, deep enough that even in the driest days there'd still be water to find."

Gabriel waited; that was clearly only the opening of the story, not the point.

"Well's never run dry, never gone sour. Old John had the Touch, you see; water came to him natural as breathing and listened when he asked it to stay. Most years, we never have to worry. Rains like the one outside, snows in the winter, the creek is enough. We're careful. But there's no sweeter water to be found, not for days."

To find and pull water in this arid land was not the simple matter Henry made it sound, but it explained how the town had been able to thrive here, rather than moving camp every season. But it still did not explain the words that had first caught his attention. "And it needs to be guarded...?"

Zacarías pursed his mouth as though he'd tasted something sour. "There are other folk who are less careful with their using."

"They're lazy, pure and simple," Henry corrected. "Rather take than make, and they don't see a need to pay for what they take. Water, sheep, rugs... it's all the same to them."

"Bandits," Gabriel guessed, and when both men nodded, he sighed. "I ran into one of theirs a few days back, I think. She didn't give me any trouble, but I'd been hoping I was heading away from their camp, not toward."

"They're well northeast of us most of the time, keeping to where the Road passes. Most time, they leave us be," Zacarías said. "But the well holds a fascination for them I do not understand."

"We told you why," Henry said, and either didn't see or ignored the expression on Zacarías' face, a faint sniff of disbelief, or doubt. "The purity of the water isn't by chance," he explained to Gabriel. "Old John wasn't one to take chances, so when they started digging, and again when the water came in, he got an elder and some of his water-dancers to come in and bless it. Supposed to keep the haints from spoiling the water, making anyone sick. And yes, I saw you make that face, Zacarías. Old John would've had you do a pass over it as well, if you'd been here then. He didn't play favorites. There's no wisdom in taking chances, not with water. Not out here."

Gabriel hrmmmed his agreement. He'd never had to worry about the water he drank; a simple touch told him if it was unsafe, and he'd never really paused to think about it, even when he was teaching Isobel to do the same. But not everyone had the Touch, and in a town of any size, even with a creek nearby.... Too many things could go wrong, too many people could die quickly, if the well went bad.

A town—or a large enough camp.

"So, the bandits, they want access to your well."

Henry's face twisted unpleasantly, his sharp-pointed beard twitching. "If it were that simple, we'd share with them and no begrudging. They want the entire town."

6

After he'd finished his meal, as though putting down his bowl was a silent signal, other residents of Rabbit's Mound came over, singly and in pairs, occasionally accompanied by children, to be introduced. Gabriel did his best to greet them politely, struggling to remember names with the faces. But once warm, fed, and dried, exhaustion set in, and when a yawn escaped him, practically cracking his jaw, the old man who'd been recounting a story of the early days of the town stopped, then slapped a surprisingly strong hand on his shoulder.

"And there's the hind leg of a donkey talked off, just like my momma warned."

Gabriel felt himself blushing. "I'm sorry, I—"

"No, no, you're a guest and we're showing pitiful hospitality, jawing at you while you're nearly dead on your feet."

He looked around the hall, summoning Henry back from where he was talking with another man. Gabriel noted that most of the folk had cleared their tables and left, only a few adults and the scattering of dogs remaining.

"Your boy needs his bed," the old man said to Henry. Gabriel might have been offended at the demotion to boy at his age, but they both had at least a decade on him, and likely more, so he let it pass.

"Too late to try and foist you onto someone," Henry decided. "We've not guesthouses as such, but there's a loft over where we left your beast, should be dry and warm and comfortable enough if you don't mind the smell of horse and hay. You being a Rider, I'm suspecting you don't."

He did not.

They said goodnight to the older man and walked back to the shed, where Henry pointed out the ladder to the loft, and left him with a promise of a fresh-cooked breakfast in the morning.

The other horse had been taken somewhere while they were eating dinner, and Steady seemed almost pathetically glad to see him, shoving his blunt head against Gabriel's shoulder, then lipping at his hair.

"Stop that, you idiot." Gabriel ran a hand through his hair and grimaced at the slight slobbers that came away in his fingers. "Look like they took good care of you." There was fresh water in the trough, and the remains of grain, and Steady had that sleepy look in his eye he got after a full meal. "Not your usual accommodations, hey? Not mine either, truth be told. But it seems well enough, and it's dry, which is more than I was expecting a few hours ago."

He gave the horse another once-over with his hands, making sure there wasn't any swelling or lumps he might've missed when unsaddling him earlier.

"All right, you look fine. I'm going to crawl up there," and he jerked a thumb at the ladder built into the wall, "and get some shuteye. Anyone comes knocking, probably best you don't trample them, okay?"

The loft wasn't quite high enough for him to stand upright, with an unprotected edge overlooking the lower level that gave him pause, but there was a small oil lamp that cast a pleasant glow, and the floor was layered with more worn rugs for sleeping, with room for him to stash his pack and lay out his bedroll.

"I need to find out what they're wanting for one of these rugs," he said, pulling off his boots and settling in for the night. "Maybe two." Never mind that carrying one would be useless excess, even if he'd kept the mule.

Comfortably settled, Gabriel turned down the lamp and closed his eyes. The events of the past day swirled in his head, but he had trained himself to put aside things he could do nothing about, and the sound of the rain still pelting against the roof slowly swept him to sleep.

Lights shimmered in the darkness, tiny dots shifting like mouche à feu on a summer's night, blue and green.

"There are too many." A woman's voice, low and husky. "More than before."

"That was always a risk. That was always the risk."

If the woman's voice was vaguely familiar, Gabriel would have known the man's voice on his deathbed. Isobel's 'boss', the Master of the Territory.

"Can you stop them?" The woman again, and Gabriel could almost see her, tall and slender, hair silver as a coin under lamplight. Marie, that was who, the Right Hand to Isobel's Left.

"You can damn a river, divert its flow, but you cannot stop it. This is what was always going to happen, Marie. The only question was when. And now we have the answer."

"Then the Territory is doomed."

"The Territory was always doomed, as it was. Nothing remains, when water has its way. So now we will see what comes."

"And Isobel? And us?"

A low chuckle, and the faint flickerthwack of cards being shuffled. "We do what we have always done. Change is not the end; doom is not disaster."

There was a distinctly feminine sigh, then the clink of glasses. "You're very annoying."

A door opened, then closed.

"Doom is not disaster," the devil said again, and Gabriel knew, somehow, that he was speaking directly to him. "The river runs, the mountains rise and fall, the winds shatter, and the bones... the bones remain. Remember that. The bones remain."

"GABRIEL!"

Brother Zacarías was far too cheerful, and far too loud. Gabriel groaned, draping his arm over his eyes as though that could block the other man's voice out.

"It's well past dawn, Gabriel. Arise!"

"I'm not one of your initiates, to need morning prayers and soul-scouring," he muttered, but threw back the blanket and sat up carefully, remembering the low ceiling overhead and sudden drop to his left. His body ached, but nowhere near as much as it would have sleeping on the ground, in the rain, and for that he was willing to be thankful.

"There's coffee and fresh bread waiting," the monk called up, and then there was the sound of the door opening and shutting again behind him.

Gabriel rubbed a hand over his face, feeling the rough bristles on his chin and cheeks. "And hot water for shaving, hopefully." He didn't mind looking a vagabond on the Road, but in civilized quarters it was best to look civilized, as much as he could.

He pulled on his clothes and boots and slid down the ladder, noting this morning the details he'd missed the night before: the smoothness of the wood under his hands, the evenness of the rungs, and how carefully it was set into the wall with metal pegs. They were careful with details, here in Rabbit's Mound.

Someone had brought in a fresh fodder for Steady while he slept—Zacarías, or someone else—and the horse was munching his way through it as though he'd never been stabled anywhere else.

"Don't get too used to it," he warned the horse. "We're back on the Road soon."

Steady flicked one ear dismissively and continued chewing.

SEEN IN DAYLIGHT, under a clouded-over sky, Rabbit's Mound did not look like any town he'd seen, either in the Territory or the States. The baker's dozen of houses were all small, solidly built of baked clay, with rounded corners and flat roofs, and seemed to have been scattered like a handful of grain rather than placed in any logical pattern. Not even the hunting camps he'd visited had been this... random. That seemed at odds with the details he had noted with the ladder, and the way Henry had spoken about the town' founding.

A handful of chickens pecked their way along a path, seemingly unconcerned by the human walking toward them. In the near distance he could hear voices calling, interspersed by the sharp barks of dogs, and beneath that the mutter of livestock being herded out for the day. He winced, imagining what sort of draw the animals must be for everything from coyote to Reaper hawks, and hoped their pens were well-guarded, and their shepherds well-armed.

A woman came out of one of the houses, a rope basket balanced on her hip and a floppy cloth hat perched on her head. She saw him and raised her free hand in greeting, then walked between two houses and out of sight.

"In here."

The voice came from behind him, and he turned to see Zacarías standing outside the main hall. "If you stand out there like a cow, someone will come by and milk you," the monk warned. "Come inside!"

Where the night before the hall had been crowded, this morning it was nearly empty, the tables bare and clean, the fire-pit cool, the ashes from the night before swept into a neat corner at the edge. But the kitchen was clearly still in use, from the clatter and crash he could hear from beyond the arched doorway.

"Too much went undone yesterday, because of the rains," the monk said, leading Gabriel to a table where two tin mugs waited, curls of steam rising from within. "And a few roofs were discovered to be in need of repair. I don't suppose you have any skills in that direction?"

"None whatsoever," Gabriel admitted, taking a sip of the sweetly bitter brew. It wasn't bad, although after a year of drinking Isobel's attempts at campfire coffee, his standards were no longer high. "But I'm willing to do what I can to help, in exchange for last night's boarding." He would have offered coin, but he had little left, and suspected they had little use for it out here.

Zacarías grinned, the change of expression making him look far younger than his years. "How are you at cleaning dishes?"

Which was how, after the promised breakfast of bread and surprisingly spicy sausage and greens, Gabriel found himself standing at a deep tub, dipping plates and cups into the water to rinse, and then handing them to a skinny, brown-haired girl to dry.

The girl looked at him sideways, then stared back intently at the towel in her hands. "Where you from?"

"I've been all over, but I was born in the North."

"Where it snows all the time?" She sounded as though she doubted that it did, in fact, snow at all, much less all the time.

"Not all the time, but... yes, it gets very cold and snowy in the winter."

"And there are bears?"

Gabriel felt his lip twitch and repressed it sternly. "Many bears."

"We got coyotes," she said, in the tone of someone confiding a secret. "Big ones. They'll take a sheep, iffin' we don't watch out."

"Is that so?"

"Mmmhmmm."

He tried to imagine Isobel at this age and found it surprisingly easy. She would have been just as serious-eyed, just as certain of herself. Doubts wouldn't come until later.

"I'd like to see a bear," the girl said.

"Maybe someday you will," he said, and handed her the last dish.

"But not until you are older, Mercy." Zacarías had left them to do their work but returned with suspicious timing just as they finished up. "Now, go, it's time for school."

Gabriel wiped his hands on the towel, and nodded in response to Mercy's hurried farewell, then raised an eyebrow at the monk.

"She's only eleven," Zacarías said. "Please do not fill her head with too many stories of the Road."

Gabriel laughed and shook his head. "Eleven's just the right age to start dreaming. But it's not for everyone." He'd not wanted it, himself. Not until he came back, and it had been his only option.

The monk tilted his head sideways, and in the reflecting sunlight from the open door Gabriel could see where the hair on the top of his head was shorter than the rest, his tonsure still growing in. "She has a gift for soothing those in pain. We have hopes of apprenticing her to Joseph, our chirurgeon, or a medicine woman, not lose her to wandering the Dust Roads."

The asperity in his tone startled a laugh out of Gabriel. "Take off that robe, lose the accent, there's not a thing separating you from Territory-born."

"There is part of me that is offended by that," Zacarías said. "But... I did choose to remain."

Gabriel folded the abandoned dishtowel over the sink's edge to dry, and crossed his arms, leaning against the wall. "Why did you? Last we saw of your folk, you were heading back over the Knife, disgusted by the ways and mores of us dissolute Territory folk. And yet, here you are. Don't tell me you thought you could save the souls of the Territory all by yourself?"

Zacarías affected a most pious expression, folding his hands together as though in prayer. "I would not be by myself, but the Lord, whose words I carry."

"Mmmm." Gabriel put all his skepticism into that single noise.

"And," Zacarías admitted, dropping his hands, "there may have been a suspicion that the Crown would not be pleased with us when we returned. While the Church protects her own, that protection is not absolute."

Considering the monks had entered the Territory without formal permission, seeking to put an end to the spell their king had ordered loosed on the Territory, Gabriel didn't doubt that there would be cause for concern.

"And your brothers?" The ones who had survived the beast, anyway.

"They..." Zacarías sighed, and shrugged, lifting his hands as though to disavow all responsibility for his former companions. "They had more faith than I. Or more foolishness. They are often two flips of the same coin, you say?"

"Sides. Two sides of the same coin."

"Ah. They returned home, and I did not. And perhaps it was God's will, after all. That I remain here, and share my faith with those who will listen, in their times of doubt and need. Just as it was God's will that we meet with you and young Isobel, to jointly finish what was needed against that hellspawn beast. And now we are together again, and perhaps there is a reason for that as well." He paused. "You scoff? Do you not believe in fate, Gabriel?"

"I really don't." Not the fate Zacarías spoke of, anyway. "But you do?"

"God works in mysterious ways, and it is not for the likes of us to question, merely obey."

Gabriel suspected his expression said what he thought of that, saving him from the rudeness of saying it. But Zacarías smiled gently, as though he'd expected nothing else from Gabriel, and was not offended.

"And your devil, he does not care that I speak of God."

"He really doesn't," Gabriel agreed to that without hesitation. The Old Man didn't care about much of anything folk did, so long as they stayed out of his hair, and didn't cause a fuss he had to deal with—or send his Hand to deal with. "You know he's not actually the devil, right?"

Zacarías gave him an odd look. "The Church is aware of that fact, yes. But he lays claim to the title and offers no other. It is not comfortable to speak, but how else does one call him?"

"Isobel calls him the boss, but I guess that won't work for you, no?"

Zacarías shook his head, that gentle smile back on his lips.

"Master of the Territory's much of a mouthful, and not accurate, either. I suppose devil will have to do."

Zacarías dipped a hand into the pocket of his robe, and drew out a delicate rope of beads, the sigil of the hanging man dangling from the end. He draped it over one palm, letting his thumb run over the beads, one by one. "It seems to me, after longer acquaintance, that the Territory is a beautiful, but very strange place."

Gabriel rubbed a hand over his jaw, reminded that he'd wanted a shave. "It really is."

Suddenly tiring of their tete-a-tete, he closed his eyes briefly, then opened them to look the other man square in the face, watching not his expression, but the movement of his eyes. "Why did Henry bring me here, Zacarías?"

The monk's face was innocent as a lamb, but his lids flickered, dark brown eyes widening just a hair, and the motion of his thumb on the bead stopped. "I do not know what you mean."

"Men of God should be better liars. I could tell he was with me on the Road before he said anything. He watched me before he spoke up, probably for a while." While the old man put up a decent façade of Unexpected Rescuer, the details didn't add up, for Gabriel, least of all the question of why had Henry been out in that storm at all? He hadn't been hunting, hadn't been traveling... there had been no sane reason to be there, save one: that he was looking for something. Or someone.

"He could have let me go, could have stayed quiet and I'd have ridden right by, but he didn't. And he brought me here, where you don't have so much as a guest-house to spare, and based on what I've seen, you barely scrape enough to feed your own.

"And then you being here?" Gabriel didn't give the monk time to form a protest. "The Territory's not infinite, but it's plenty large, and yet of all everywhere, you're here." He lifted a hand, and began ticking instances off, one per finger. "So we've a man who just happens to be out in the pouring rain, when sane folk are home safe and dry. And that man just happens to find a stranger, who is plucked off the Road and offered hospitality, despite the town being shadowed by bandits. Fair enough; some folk are that kind, I'll grant you. But in that town, it just happens is another man who knows this stranger, and his connection to the Devil's Hand, if not the devil himself."

Gabriel looked at his fingers, then closed them back into his palm.

"Coincidences happen, but, as Isobel often reminded me, the devil doesn't believe in coincidences. Says it's just bad luck we're paying attention to. And I'm thinking that bad luck is mine.

"So, tell me; why did Henry bring me here? If you were looking for Isobel, she and I don't ride together any more. She's finished her mentorship, she's out on her own now."

Zacarías looked back into the main hall as though hoping for someone to come rescue him, but the few people who had been there earlier had gone off while Gabriel was washing dishes. They could hear voices outside, rising and falling as they went about their business, but Zacarías made no attempt to summon any of them.

The monk's shoulders lifted slightly, as though to shrug, then fell again, and he tucked the wooden beads back into his pocket. "In truth, Gabriel, we did not look for you. Nor the dama Isobel, although her presence would have been.... Well." The monk gave another delicate shrug. "It was not to be."

Gabriel didn't want to get into another discussion of fate. "But Henry was out there looking for someone. Something?"

"Someone. Anyone. And not only Henry, though he was the one to find you. And not only that night. For many days now, looking. Hoping.

"You have seen the village. It is not small, but we are farmers, craftsmen, *families*, not soldiers. And we are isolated."

Gabriel was beginning to understand. "And the bandits have been circling."

"Sí. Closer and closer, like a zopilote in the sky, circling a thing that is dying, not quite ready to swoop, but biding its time, knowing that its prey cannot outrun death."

Bandits, generally, were part of the risks of living in the Territory. You'd get one or two thinking the Road was their trough, and the occasional group setting up shop somewhere, feeding off the locals. So long as they left the native tribes alone, the devil didn't seem to particularly care, leaving them to Road Marshals to clear out as needed. But marshals were few and far between; Gabriel couldn't remember the last time he'd encountered one on the Road, and the last badgehouse had been.... a long while back. Nearest marshal he knew of was Rafe, back in Red Stick. But Rafe'd set down his badge and not seemed happy to pick it up again even for trouble in his own town.

Thoughts of marshals brought a remembrance of the tree that had grown seemingly overnight, the silhouette of it against the sky so like their sigil.

Gabriel wanted to say he didn't believe in signs or portent, but he wasn't a liar. But that didn't mean he had to listen to them.

"You're looking for protection? Against an entire camp?" He thought of the woman he'd encountered, her calm self-assurance, the way she'd determined that he was neither threat nor profitable target. "You'd be better off making a deal with them for the water."

Zacarías rolled his eyes to the heavens, then gestured with one hand for Gabriel to follow him, walking from the kitchen back into the main hall. There were two old women sitting at the far end nearest the fireplace, spinning, but other than that it was now deserted. The clack clack clack of the drop-wheels was a half-forgotten sound from Gabriel's childhood, and despite himself, some measure of tension in his body eased.

"That was my thought as well, when I came here," Zacarías admitted, taking a seat on one of the wooden benches. "That reasonable men should not fight over what could be shared. But these are not reasonable men, Gabriel. They refused an offer to meet and discuss, do not come to us with an offer themselves. They only come and watch, one at a time, for days at a time. Up on the ridge, just beyond the wards.

"They do not speak, they do not attack, but they wait, and they *watch*."

"Huh." That wasn't the pattern for most bandits. They tended to be impatient bastards, quicker to swing or shoot than not. "How long's this been going on?"

"Since before I came here. A year, a little more?"

"Watching, and not talking. It's making the town nervous. And nervous men do foolish things." Gabriel was impressed by the cunning behind it, though he did not voice that thought. He ignored the bench opposite Zacarías, instead paced the space between the tables, thinking out loud. "They want, but they can't just take. Why?" He was thinking out loud to himself, not expecting the monk to answer. "If the well was blessed, likely that the entire town was, too. The wards, were they part of the original grant, Old John's agreement with the locals?"

"I do not know."

"They're on good terms, so probably. Native wardings are different things, we learned that the hard way." In the snow-town of Andreas, where Isobel had come too close to dying. He shook off the memory, forcing himself to concentrate on the now. "Even if they aren't, I'm guessing the connection means there's a part of this town that's still tied to the local tribe. So they can't attack, not without breaking Agreement and risking the devil getting involved. But all they need is one of you to break, and they can claim that you were the ones who gave offense, that they had the right to respond."

The Agreement kept the Territory intact, despite the seemingly endless waves of settlers arriving every year; it taught the newcomers how to behave while they learned to survive. But like any law, you could bend it if you were smart enough, foolish enough. And maybe not today, maybe not next week, but eventually, someone in the town was going to do something foolish. That was just how people *were*.

He'd seen Isobel mediate a situation like this, keep it from getting worse. Well, not quite like this, but alike enough to be precedent. But he was no Hand to give and enforce judgement. Isobel was the one who should have been drawn to ride this way, not him.

"It's not a pleasant situation you've come to," he told the monk. "I wish you luck in figuring it out."

7

The conversation died down into an awkward silence, after that. They'd had things in common, but those things were in the past, and there was little more to say. Gabriel, after asking for Henry's direction, left Zacarías to whatever it was the monk did during the day and went in search of the older man. He reached into his pocket as he walked, jingling the silver bits there. It should be enough. He'd thank the old man for the night's lodging, hand over a few coins to consider his debt paid, and ride on.

Outside the dining hall, Gabriel paused to take his bearings, nodding politely at the few folk who walked by. The shed where Steady was stabled was at his right elbow, the double doors open, allowing the morning sunlight to enter, a rope gate tied across to keep the animal within. Not that Steady was prone to wandering; he'd trained the gelding too well for that. Especially if there was grain and water where he was.

Ahead of him, the clay-and-stone houses he'd noted earlier were grouped three or four in a clump, with well-trod paths snaking around them. Bursts of color appeared seemingly at random, clumps of flowering plants and bright-painted marker-posts set along the walls and pathways. He'd learned during dinner the night before that each family group had a house to themselves where they slept, but the meals were mostly taken together in the Hall, and there were several bathing houses scattered throughout the town, to conserve water during the dry summer months.

Henry's home was distinguishable from the others only by the mosaic of stones set over the doorway, a circle of pale blue. A woman, a tiny bird of a thing, silvered hair tied up in a neat knot, had been working in her palm-sized garden outside when Gabriel walked up, and remained there after calling her husband to join them, her brown eyes wide and watchful.

"Thank you, Greta," Henry said, and dropped a kiss on the back of her hand before turning to look Gabriel up and down. "You're looking better than you did last night."

"Considerably less damp, at least," Gabriel agreed, smiling easily. But when he offered the coin, Henry looked down his nose and pushed Gabriel's hand away. "We've no use for your coin. We could use your help, though."

Gabriel sighed, shifting uncomfortably. "I've already had this talk with Zacarías. One man's not going to be enough to save you, not if the bandits decide they want your town. Maybe a marshal, if one came your way." Rafe, or Isobel, if this were truly a matter for the devil. He could give them her direction; they could send a call for her, if she were still in town, or chase after her...

But even the Hand couldn't be everywhere. If the devil didn't send her or the Territory call her, if there was no under-lying illness like she'd been drawn to before, would she even come? *Could* she?

"I'm sorry. I can't help you." He refused to feel guilty; this wasn't anything he'd signed on for.

"Then we are doomed."

Gabriel knew when he was being manipulated; Henry

wasn't even trying to be subtle. "You need a marshal for this. Or... You could send a message to Flood," he said. "The devil—"

"The devil has more important things to worry about than one small town in the middle of nowhere," Henry said, and since Gabriel had been thinking much the same thing, he couldn't argue.

"Brother Zacarías says that you rode with the Devil's Hand."

"I did." And then before the older man could say anything, he shook his head. "I was her mentor on the Road, nothing more. I've no call or claim on her, and I've no knowledge of where she is, now. Last I saw her, she was in Red Stick." He suspected that without him she would return to Flood, her mentorship ride complete, and once there the devil would do with her as he would. "Have you requested the aid of the,"" and he racked his brain to remember the name of the nearest tribe, "the Tua?"

Greta made a rude noise, and Henry threw up his hands. "Request them to do what? Stand with us against white men? White men who have given them no offense—have given *us* no offense, yet, save that they make us deeply uncomfortable, and make no secret of the fact that they covet what we have?"

Gabriel inclined his head with a faint grimace.

A marshal would say much the same, that no action had been taken, and the Law needs action to react. They would be sympathetic, of course, and maybe even deeply concerned, but useless.

"We had hoped you..."

Henry's voice tailed off, and Gabriel ran a hand through his hair in frustration. "That I would what? What could one man do, that a town could not?"

"We're farmers here, farmers and herders and crafters. Our hunting skills are best left to rabbits and fending off the occasional coyote. We are the rabbits, here. Or worse, sheep huddled in a herd and ready for clipping."

There was absolutely nothing Gabriel could say to that; it was all true.

"I'm not a soldier."

"This is not a war. It is a trap, and we are already caught in it." Henry frowned, then looked back at Greta, who had turned her back on the both of them at some point, carefully picking over the palm-sized garden in front of their door, plucking leaves off the winter greens, one at a time. "I ask you, please reconsider."

"I'm sorry."

"As am I." Henry reached out with his hand, offering it to shake, and Gabriel took it, his eyes widening as he felt something sharp and hot engulf his palm, racing down his fingers and up his arm.

"What?" He tried to pull away, but Henry held fast.

"I'm sorry," Henry said again. "But we need you."

GABRIEL WAS FURIOUS. He'd blistered Henry's ears, left and right, and the man had stood there and taken it, but refused to break the binding. Teeth gritted, Gabriel had stalked back to where Steady was stabled, had thrown the saddle over the gelding's back, lashed his pack with hand that shook with rage, and ridden out.

Whatever Henry had used to bind him, it was effective; the moment he crossed the town's border wards, his body clenched so hard he nearly fell off the gelding's back, and the further he went, the harder it became to breathe.

"Arseworm. Villain. Shitgoblet." Gabriel tried to remember every rude phrase he'd ever heard, spitting them out as he tried to push Steady further. But the gelding could tell something was wrong with his rider, and balked, no matter how hard

Gabriel but his heels to his side. If he'd a switch, he might have been tempted to use it on the beast, jut to take one step more.

"Fine. Then I'll do it on my own." He slipped form the saddle, barely hanging on to the reins as he did so and crumpled to his knees.

"This isn't pain," he gritted, willing himself to believe it. "I've scratches worse than this." The marks on his face, still visible when he shaved, from when the ghost-cat had attacked him. The scars on his torso, from the spell-beast. The crick in his knee, from when Flatfoot had kicked him hard enough he'd not been able to ride for a week. All those things had been pain. This was nothing.

He got to his feet, pressing a fist against his chest, still pulling at Steady's reins with the other hand, and took one step. Then another. A third, and the pain began to ebb, just slightly, giving him the strength to take another step.

He had lost count by the time the pain faded, and he was able to breathe again.

"Drown you and your bindings," he muttered, rubbing at his chest as though that could erase the soreness there, or the rawness in his throat. He turned back to Steady, gripping the horse's mane to steady himself, then pulling his body back into the saddle.

"The bandits can have them and be welcome."

He kicked Steady into a gentle trot, and they went a dozen paces before he reined the horse in again, swearing more quietly under his breath. He half expected to hear the slithering laughter of the spirit-snake at Steady's hooves, but there was nothing but the sound of his own still-labored breathing, and Steady's gentle huffs.

"Ahh..." He turned the horse and rode back the way he'd come.

NO-ONE STOPPED him as he rode back into town, the border wards barely a brush against his skin this time. He unsaddled Steady and gave him a rub-down, less because the horse needed it and more because he did not trust himself to speak with anyone in this town without violence.

"You are angry."

Of course they'd send the monk to plead their case. Gabriel rested the flat brush against Steady's neck, and exhaled, working his throat before he could get the words out. "It is, generally, the appropriate reaction to being restrained against your will and without cause, yes."

He had broken the binding, but the offense remained, and he was not ready to let that go. Would likely never let that go, and better Henry—and all concerned—know that from the start.

"He had cause. That is not to excuse it, but... he had cause. He is afraid. And you were a prayer of hope he could not bear to let go."

"I assume that you're praying for his soul, for such hubris."

"I pray for all our souls, for that and more reasons. And I will not ask you to forgive him."

"Good."

"But until the spell wears off, will you not at least consider our request?"

"I broke the binding," he said flatly. Then, "Ours?"

"Henry speaks for all of us, by election, even if he does not always act as we might approve."

Gabriel turned to say something, just in time to see Zacarías frown. "Although I suspect there are many who would not... disapprove. This has been going on for nearly a year, and they are near to desperate, Gabriel. You said so yourself, that nervous men do foolish things."

"Damn it..." Gabriel started to throw the brush onto the ground, then checked himself, tucking it back into the pack instead. He'd studied Law back in the States, too many years ago, and the main thing he'd taken from it was that desperate men were as dangerous to themselves as others. Desperate, foolish, and with enough Touch to work binding spells was a disaster waiting to happen.

The bandits doubtless knew this, too. Although perhaps not the bit about the binding spells...

Zacarías's frown deepened. "That look in your eye. I know that look. It is the look of a man who is thinking dangerous things."

The monk looked vaguely disapproving now, and Gabriel was tempted to tell him that such looks only made people more inclined to sin, not less. Instead, he replied, "There're no thoughts worth having that aren't dangerous."

He had an idea that might end this situation peacefully. But before he said anything to Henry, Gabriel needed to see the situation for himself.

"You said that the bandits were watching the town. From where?"

It took a second for the monk to respond to the change of topic. "Up on the ridge, behind the field. Not every day. They come sometime during the night, and are there in the morning, then gone by evening."

"And they stand there, in clear view."

"Yes."

"Mmm. All right. I'm going to take a little walk, let myself think some more dangerous thoughts. Tell Henry I might have an answer for him, later tonight. And tell him come prepared to grovel for my forgiveness, while he's at it."

Zacarías made a slight movement with his hand, as though he were about to make a gesture over Gabriel, then stopped himself. "Be careful," he said, instead.

Gabriel touched his own hand to the hilt of his knife, secure in its holster. "I'm always careful, Brother."

8

Gabriel made his way through the town, noting the location of the schoolhouse where boisterous voices were rising in lessons, as well as what must be the bathhouse, a squat shape with a central chimney letting out steady puffs of white smoke. After too many years of bathing in cold rivers and stale water buckets, Gabriel had no patience with folk who scorned being clean as frivolous, or unhealthy. If they survived this, he would be making use of it, possibly for an entire day.

But first...

First, he needed information. An idea was only that, an idea. He needed facts to see if it would work.

The field Zacarías had mentioned was beyond the houses, where the creek fed into the town. The ridge would rise beyond that. Gabriel looked up, past the low roofs, then turned slightly to the left.

"There you are." The ridge barely earned the name, but he could see the slope rising, the sky a wide pale blue swathe behind it, and if he squinted he could see a shape that might have been a man, standing just at the crest.

"And how much of us can you see from up there, hmmmm?"

Just beyond the last of the houses, where several young girls were minding even younger children, there was a low barn and paddock, the smell informing him that this was where they kept their animals when they weren't out in pasture. Beyond that, marching the boundary of the town, were the fields where they grew their shared crops. Just past that he could see a shallow creek, the water meandering in a slow pattern along its muddy bed.

Gabriel paused a moment to consider the field, currently covered with some kind of leafy plant. Skirting the edges carefully, his nose picked up the unmistakable smell of damp soil underneath the vegetation. Without willing it, his senses stretched out and down, finding the tendrils of water underground, feeling the slow trickle up from deep within the bones of the earth, cool and scented with flint and dusty sage.

The well drew from these same sources, but Gabriel could not feel it.

A prickle of fear ran like spider legs up and down his arms.

"It's a tool, nothing more." His voice caught and cracked on the last word. A tool. What he did with it was up to him.

He pushed a little further, and felt only cool stone and damp earth, and a subtle, delicate resistance. The blessing Henry spoke of had been a warding of some kind, to keep the source hidden. Wise, but even the best wardings could not hide usage, and that was what had drawn the bandits' attention.

Aware that the girls had paused to watch him, a stranger in their midst, he tipped his hat in acknowledgement and walked on. There was a simple plank bridge visible further down the creek, but he would have to walk away from his destination and then back again, to use it. If it hadn't rained the night before, he might have been able to ford it without difficulty, but the water level was just high enough to make that uncomfortable.

A curve in the bank closer-by had been carved into a deeper turn, large stones placed in a half-circle to create a harbor where fish might rest during higher currents, the easier for catching. The flick and ripple of the surface told him something lived there even now, moving slow.

He had a sudden flash of a much larger shape, ripples of a more worrying size, and he ruthlessly quashed the memory. This was a scarce trickle, far away; the Mudwater could not reach him through it; the water here came from distant snowmelt and underwater springs, and it had no spirit-soul within it.

He hoped.

Looking around, he noted that the creek narrowed just below the fish-eddy, the banks coming close enough together that a solid leap would take him across. Checking to make sure that the ground was dry and solid enough that he would not slip, Gabriel braced himself, took a deep breath, and pushed off, muttering a brief prayer to any kind spirit that might be listening that he would land squarely on the other side, and not in the creek, or on his backside.

The ground came up too fast, and he landed not on his feet but his knees, the toes of his boot digging into the edge of the bank, his hands scrabbling in the dirt for balance.

He half expected to feel a hand on his shoulder, Isobel's soft voice uttering a dry commentary, and he let his forehead rest against the back of his hands for a breath before hauling himself back to his feet. Risking a glance over his shoulder, he was relieved to see that if the girls had been watching, they'd been polite enough to look away and stifle their giggles.

Gabriel did not consider himself a prideful man, but there were some things that needed no audience.

Once across the creek, the breeze picked up slightly, kicking up brief swirls of dust and grit, his boots kicking up their own puffs of dust as he walked away from the creek.

Gabriel brushed the dirt from his legs and then rubbed it from his hands before tying his kerchief over his mouth and nose and pulling his hat down low to protect his eyes. The soil here smelled dryer, the previous night's rain leaving cracks where it had sunk into the ground and disappeared, but the sere ground was broken here and there by patches of delicate flowers, pale pink petals brightening a bed of paler green.

"Lady's Love," he told Isobel, who wasn't there to hear him. They had no medical use and were bitter enough to taste that not even a mule would graze on them, but they grew seemingly overnight given even a hint of moisture. Insects clustered to them when they bloomed, and birds flocked to the insects.

Everything had a use and a purpose. He heard his father's voice for the first time in decades, low and firm in his ear as they'd watched an otter slip into the waters, its fur a gleaming brown coat. Gabriel had been a terrible hunter as a child, too easily distracted, but he'd listened to his father, and learned. His steps became softer, his breathing quieter, his thoughts softer, until he felt as small and gentle as that carpet of Lady's Love, harmless and of-the-place, that nothing should be startled by him. And step by step, he moved up the ridge at an angle, not bothering to hide, confident that he was not seen.

He was halfway up the ridge when he felt a shiver run through him, a crackling sensation like muted thunder rolling from the soles of his feet through to the crown of his head. He paused, letting the feeling settle.

He had not felt the wards when he tried to leave town that morning, the binding on him overwhelming everything else, and they had only been a mild shiver when he rode back in. But they were clear now, warning him that he had stepped beyond their protections, leaving him open to haints and demons and anything else of malign intent.

The wards were treating him as a member of the town. He

wondered briefly if Henry had set them to do that, or if they had decided on their own.

"Thank you," he said out loud, adding trade-sign for gratitude. Some might mock the idea of speaking to a ward, and even a few year ago Gabriel might have felt the same. But he'd seen and felt too much since then; the idea of wards as *aware* no longer seemed laughable.

He took another step, and then paused, half-anticipating the return of that chest-crushing pressure, the binding resurrecting itself. But other than a faint tightness in his chest, nothing happened.

"Drown you and your intentions," he muttered again, tugging his hat down more firmly over his forehead and resolutely *not* rubbing his arms against the lingering chill before starting forward once again.

The figure at the top of the ridge was still there, planted as firmly as a hundred-year oak, all his attention focused on the town below them. He had no idea that Gabriel had come up on his blind side.

Gabriel grinned tightly, unamused. People looked straight ahead, and they looked up, but they only looked down when they were uncertain of their steps, or worried about snakes.

Do not think of snakes he thought hard, as though the thought might summon them, either physical or spirit-form. For all his life, it might well, and he had no attention to spare for that nonsense, now.

Sliding slowly back to his knees, then down to his elbows, Gabriel rested on the ground with his chin resting on the backs of his hands. If he'd brought his carbine, he could have taken the man's fool head off without risk; if he slid forward even a length more, he'd have a decent chance at throwing his knife square into the man's back—or his heart, if he gave him warning enough to turn around. But killing him was not the point.

The bandit was male, younger than Gabriel but not by much based on the scrabble of beard and weathered cheek visible under his hat. He wasn't trying to hide, standing with his hands shoved into the pockets of his coat, chin jutted up and hat tilted down to make an unavoidable silhouette to anyone looking up from the town. His horse, a rangy roan, was picketed a few feet away, saddled for fast riding rather than a long trail. The bandit didn't do anything, didn't look around or make notes; for all that Gabriel could tell, he had fallen asleep on his feet, or been planted there like a marker post.

Gabriel watched for a while, letting the sun move over his back, the faint breezes swirling dust around and over him until he was coated with it, insects buzzing at his ears and hair in idle curiosity. Finally, in response to something Gabriel could not see or hear, the bandit shifted, rocking back and forth on his heels before turning back to his horse. He patted its neck and untied its reins, then swung into the saddle with a grunt that Gabriel could feel, even from that distance.

"No carbine or bow on you, nor even a spyglass," Gabriel said, easing himself into a sitting position with a pained grunt of his own. "You don't care about seeing what's going on down there at all, do you? And you're confident that nobody in that town is a threat to you."

Confidence was good. Confidence, they could use.

BY THE TIME Gabriel returned to town, crossing over the creek with even less grace than before, the sky had gone from pale blue to dark red as the sun dropped past the horizon. The air smelled like smoke and something sweeter, like burnt honey. He poked his head into the Hall, where people had gathered around the tables for the evening meal but saw neither Henry nor Zacarías.

"Excuse me?" He stopped one of the boys running trays from the kitchen. "I'm looking for—"

Before he could finish, the boy pointed out the door, then tapped his nose, and grinned. "Follow the smoke."

"Thank you."

Going back outside, he followed the smell away from the hall to a courtyard of sorts where a small bonfire had been built, the source of both smells rising from it. Nine figures waited by the fire, a handful standing together in a cluster, the rest seated on wooden stumps rough-shaped into benches. He recognized Henry, and Zacarías' long brown robes, but the others were strangers to him. Town elders, he supposed, although as he drew closer, he saw that many of them were not greybeards, but surprisingly young, and several of them were female.

"Mister Kasun." One of the men turned as Gabriel approached, holding out his hand in welcome "My name is Benjamin. I'm the schoolmaster here in Rabbit's Mound."

Gabriel took the offered hand, feeling a firm, callused grip shake once, then used that grip to draw Gabriel closer to the fire before letting go. "This –is—well, we're Town Council, such as it is."

Elected, or at least shoved into the position, then. "You make the decisions for everyone?" Zacarías had said that Henry did, but...

"We make suggestions for the town," one of the women corrected him. She was tiny, with pale skin that had clearly seen too much sun over the years, but her grip was as firm as Benjamin's, and her wide brown eyes were bright as a sparrow's, even in the firelight. "Then they decide if they're going to listen to us or not. I'm Margaret."

He was introduced to the rest of the council in succession, long-ago training making him tuck away their names and appearances and, when given, their occupations for later possible need.

"Henry said that you'd gone to take a closer look at the... situation."

"Did he now." Gabriel wondered if he'd also told them that Henry had used a binding to keep him here, that he was not doing it out of the rightness of his heart. One glance at the older man, his gaze looking somewhere off to the left, told him he hadn't.

"And did you?" Joad was the lead baker, an anxious-seeming man with a strong look of the Tenocha southlands to him, but not a trace of accent.

"You definitely have a watcher," he agreed. "And from the look of his gear, and himself, I'd agree; they're not law-abiding folk." If he'd run into that observer on the Road, he might have kept riding through the night rather than share a camp with him. Not that he'd any sense they'd not respect hospitality law, but he'd a suspicion, and oft enough, suspicion was all you got.

"We knew that already." Soren, who hadn't given an occupation. Young, likely still green and impatient with it. "If that's all you have to add—"

"Soren." It was only his name, quietly spoken, but the young man ducked his head, stepping back to let the one who'd reprimanded him come forward.

"And having seen with your own eyes and your own senses, Rider, do you have anything to add to what we already knew?" The woman who had spoken was not old; she was ancient, hair the grey of fog, skin wrinkled as a dried apple, leaning on a thick wooden cane. Gabriel fought the instinctive urge to bend in her presence, like a child leaning at a grandmother's chair, then gave way to it, removing his hat and ducking his head.

"I do, if you will hear me," he responded, echoing her formality.

"That is what we are gathered here for. I am called Rachel. Come sit with us and speak what you have to say."

It wasn't the studied formality of a courtroom, nor the fluid tradition he'd observed in native gatherings of this sort, but something else, something equally important, and Gabriel reminded himself to step carefully. These people wanted a protector, a guardian, and Henry at least was not above tricks to get it. While he'd made the choice to return and help them, he had no desire to take on an entire bandit camp, with or without their dubious aid. He needed to be careful to say only what he intended to say, and not what they wanted to hear from him.

There was a stout chair set close by the fire, and Rachel sank into it with a little sigh, resting her cane next to her, within easy reach. He had the thought that, as ancient as she was, she would be able to lay that across someone's backside with surprising strength, if need be.

There were a scattering of stools and smaller chairs as well, clearly brought out from the houses for this meeting, and he watched as most seated themselves, leaning forward to hear what he had to say.

This close to the bonfire he could identify the sweet smell as something herbal, and from the bright-colored shapes rising from the flames, likely medicinal as well as ceremonial. Lifting the now-dusty kerchief back to his nose would be rude, but he took a position upwind from the fire, so that the risk of inhaling the intoxicants was less.

"You already know what they want," he said, not bothering to ease into anything. "You also know that they have no claim to take, only to request that you share."

"They're bandits," Henry reminded him, as though he'd somehow forgotten that fact. "They have no respect for claims, or Law, only what they can take."

"If that were true, they would already be in your town, living in your houses," Gabriel retorted. "The fact that they're playing this game proves that they know the –rules—mayhap even better than you."

Henry looked as though he wanted to respond but something in Gabriel's expression must have reminded him that the rider was still sore over the attempted binding, and he shut his mouth with an almost audible snap.

"They will not dare start anything," Joad said into the pause, but the way he clasped his hand together, almost in prayer, suggested he didn't believe that.

Before Gabriel could respond to that foolishness, Margaret jumped in. "They're just waiting for the right moment. When we're distracted, or down with the grippe the way we were three winters past and can't defend ourselves."

"Our wardings—"

"Aren't enough!" Samael, head of the weaving family, had been quiet until now. "You've seen how they keep moving closer, taunting us. They're not afraid—"

"They're not afraid, no," Gabriel broke into the rising agitation, pitching his voice to carry without shouting. "But they're not going to attack. And not because of your wardings, because you're right; it would slow them down, make them uncomfortable, but it won't stop them." Not even the Mudwater or the Knife can stop a determined host, just dissuade them. "But they're not going to attack because they don't have to, not with the game they're playing."

"The Agreement—" Joad protested, and the third woman, a healer named Althea who had introduced herself as Mercy's mother, nodded her head vigorously in support.

"Let Gabriel speak," Henry said when Samael started to argue. "Joad, Sam, let the man speak."

Gabriel pressed his hands together, palm to palm, and lifted them to his mouth, trying to shape his word before he spoke them.

"I've ridden the Dust Roads most of my adult life. I've

shared camp hospitality with all sort of folk, some law-abiding, some not. I know how they think. And before that, I was an advocate. Back in the States." He waited, gaze moving around the group to make sure they all understood what that meant. He had been trained to argue all comers, from all corners of both Law and practice.

"Brother Zacarías can confirm that I was the mentor to the Devil's Left Hand this past year. I've seen how she thinks, and how deep the devil moves." he thought of the dream-vision he'd had. *The bones remain.* He still did not understand what the devil meant, not entirely, but Isobel's boss could see a larger picture, could see corners of the map that Gabriel could not.

"Trust me," he said now, to the folk in front of him. "These bandits know what they are doing, and they have no plans to attack your town unprovoked. They don't have to. You're going to open the gate for them yourselves."

He crossed his arms and waited for the renewed babble of voices to die down. Behind them, the bonfire blazed, sparks crackling into the darkening air, the burst of sweet herbs filling his nostrils, no matter how he tried to turn. He didn't think they'd use anything that fogged the senses, but the shapes forming and twisting within the fire were too disturbing to look at for very long, making him feel uncomfortable things. Everything he knew of science told him that salamanders were not beasts born of flame, and yet, every time he let a flicker catch his gaze, he could see a long, lean body stretching out on the log, red-flame tongue and soot-colored eye before the fire swept over it again.

Eventually, the voices died away, their indignation dying for lack of response or fuel.

"Explain yourself," Henry said, then added, grudgingly, "please."

It was the reverse of the game the devil was playing. "They are provoking you. Watching in plain view, knowing that you can see them, without any sense of what they intend? They do that to make you uneasy, suspicious.

"They know that they cannot attack, for all the reasons you have said. But by skirting at the edges, playing on your fears? They're prodding at your worst instincts, taking advantage of every bump and hitch in your thoughts. And they'll keep doing that until you stop speaking, and swing. And then they will be the wronged ones."

"And at that point, we would have no grounds to call a marshal when they did attack," the old woman said. Resignation and bitterness was heavy in her voice, making him think that she'd encountered marshals before, and it had not ended well.

Fair enough; marshals were only mortal, and some worse than others.

"You could certainly call, and I could tell you the names of some to trust, but by the time one got here, likely the only recourse he'd have would be to take them before a judge and hope he ruled in your favor."

Rachel scowled, but did not disagree.

"So, you would have us ignore them? That if they cannot provoke us, they will go away?" Samael sounded rightfully dubious about that strategy.

Gabriel could only shrug. "An old teacher of mine once told me that the only way to avoid conflict is to remove yourself from it. To go where it can no longer reach you." This wasn't what Graciendo had been thinking of, but Gabriel thought the advice still fit.

Henry shook his head. "We will not abandon our town."

There was a mutter of agreement, and Gabriel inclined his head in unsurprised acknowledgement. "Then you will, eventually, take the bait. It's no insult to any of you or your kin; there's only so far a man can be pushed, even knowing he's being pushed, before he pushes back, and the longer he resists, the bloodier things will be."

Henry looked as though he'd eaten something sour, his pale skin ruddy-cast in the firelight. "No matter what we do, we lose."

"Mayhap not." Gabriel's mouth quirked up in an unhappy smile. "Not if you push them to action first."

Soren perked his head up at that. "You have a plan."

"It's more of a terrible idea than a plan, but... yes."

PASSIM

There was bone and there was wind, and there was water. From bone came the world, and from the wind came medicine, and from water came the things that lived, and grew, and died.

And together they shaped the Dust Road, that all walk for a span of time...

9

"Go on. Say it."

"Say what?"

"Whatever it is that you've been wanting to say all evening."

Zacarías lifted both eyebrows and widened his eyes to create the appearance of heartfelt innocence. Gabriel tore a strip of bread off the loaf on the table in front of them and ran it through the juice remaining from his dinner, sopping up the last bits of chicken with it. They'd stayed at the bonfire, hammering out the details, for hours, and by the time they returned the tables were cleared and the kitchen gone quiet. Thankfully, there had been food left for them by the hearth, the fire keeping it reasonably warm.

"There is nothing to say. This plan of yours is madness, and we are madmen for considering it, but we were madmen as well when we stood against the beast made of spell-malice, you and I, and that worked. Principalmente."

"Mostly." And it had worked because Isobel had been with them, Isobel and the magician Farron. "We may all die."

Zacarías blinked at him, still holding onto that façade of

innocence. "We may all die at any moment, Gabriel. I have long since made my peace with my Lord."

"Well, I haven't," Henry said from his seat lower at the table, his face set in a scowl. "So, I'd appreciate if we try very hard not to die."

"Seconded," Samael said, and an echo of 'ayes' went around the table.

Gabriel looked at Zacarías and raised his own eyebrows in challenge. "We may need to live, Brother."

"If it is God's Will, we shall."

Gabriel shook his head, biting back a reluctant chuckle. The plan itself was simple. Foolish beyond belief, and likely to fail, but simple: bring the bandits into the town itself, and push them to give direct offense, enough to threaten the town's existence, in the hope of redirecting the devil's –attention—and through him, his Hand. And then using the threat of –that— and Gabriel's own relationship with her as the –whip—to force them to back off.

It was a terrible idea and a worse plan. There were too many ifs, too many places where it could splinter and fail. But if the bandits would not leave and the town would not give way, it was the only plan Gabriel could come up with.

And since none of the others had anything better, they had agreed.

BENJAMIN HAD THE NEATEST HAND, and so it fell to him to craft the message, Henry leaning over his shoulder to dictate the word, occasionally looking up at Gabriel for correction.

It was an invitation, a safe-pass for five members of the bandit's camp to enter town under a flag of parley, to discuss the matter of the well, and access thereof.

"Five is too many," Joad had said, unhappy. "Why can they not just send one, who can speak for them?"

"Would you send a single member of your town into the home of those who might harm him?" Zacarías, surprisingly, was the one to respond. "One, they would refuse. Two even—two are easily ambushed. Three, perhaps?"

"Five," Gabriel said. "Three suggests that we fear them coming into our town. Four is an unlucky number. Five allows them to feel confident, but also tells them that we are comfortable with five in our midst."

"Then why not six?"

A year of living with Isobel's pungent side-eye had allowed Gabriel to imitate it to near-perfection, and he turned it on Margaret now.

"Five, then." Benjamin had inked the words, then sanded and sealed the note with careful hands, ending all debate.

A cloth envelope, waterproofed with wax, was produced, and the message placed within, then the next morning, one of the older boys in the village was summoned to carry it to the ridge where Gabriel had watched the bandit watching the town, left there for whoever came next to find.

"They'll ignore a young boy, if they even see him," Henry had said when Benjamin objected to using one of the children that way. "And it's not as though the girls didn't regularly bring the goats up that way, before all this started. No harm will come to the child, Benjamin, and he'll be back in time for classes, worse luck for the boy."

THE COUNCIL TOOK turns observing the ridge, taking casual walks along the creek, or checking the field or flock. That first day, no observer came, but the morning after, Soren saw the silhouette of a figure appear—and then disappear.

The next afternoon, five figures appeared on the other side of the creek. Three men and two women, all mounted on horses the image of the roan Gabriel had seen before, raw-boned and blunt-headed, as alike to his own Steady they could have been taken from the same herd.

Road-horses. That wasn't to say these bandits had been Riders, before... but it increased the odds.

Gabriel wasn't sure what that told him, but it was a detail, and every detail was important.

"You wanted to talk, we're here to talk!" one of the men called out. He'd a northern accent, Gabriel noted; the broadly rounded A and flattened R familiar from his own childhood. A ways from home, but he supposed you rarely turned bandit in your own yard.

Henry cast a sideways glance at Gabriel, who nodded without taking his attention from the bandits.

"You're welcome to cross the river in accordance with the terms of parley, and in good faith of the Devil's Agreement," the older man called in response.

Calling the creek a river was foolishness, but foolishness with a purpose. You call like to like and giving something power meant it would pay attention. Running water was proof against some spells and bindings, but not all. Hopefully, what-ever they'd thought to bring in with them—and none of the council was fool enough to think they wouldn't try—would be washed away.

Hedging their own bet, Gabriel'd had Henry place a binding on their side of the bank where they'd invited them to cross. Nothing overt, nothing a medicine-worker or even an alert Rider would notice, but if Gabriel was –right—and he wasn't at all sure he – riding over it would bind them to any agreed—upon terms, even if they meant to break them.

Of course, bindings didn't mean much if they carried their

own bindings on them. And just naming the creek a river didn't actually *give* the water that power...

Which was why none of them were relying on it.

The riders crossed the creek en masse, the horse's hooves churning up mud in ways that looked deliberate. Beside him, Gabriel heard Joad mutter a curse, doubtless thinking of how that mud would affect everything downstream.

"Don't," he said, keeping his lips a still as possible. "They're trying to rile you. Don't let 'em."

There was no sign of any more bandits lurking up the ridge, and the road into town had clear visibility a mile down, with nowhere for a would-be attacker to hide. If the bandits had brought reinforcements, they weren't within sudden ambush range. But Gabriel slipped the tie on his knife holster and loosed the blade in his boot, just the same. Bringing the enemy into the heart of your town was an act of –confidence—but also one of idiocy.

Joad led the group through town to the hall, with Gabriel taking up the rear. He saw the looks the bandits gave him as they passed by, saw them take in his holster, the set of his arms, and acknowledge it: if something were to happen, they would go for him first. Not ideal, but better than the alternatives.

With luck, it would never become an issue.

The woman who'd visited his campsite was among the riders. Interesting. He watched her as she settled herself at the table in the hall, but even with the once-over they'd given him, she gave no sign of recognition. He supposed that was to be expected; he'd not looked his best at that moment, and he'd slept, bathed and shaved since then. Besides, there was no reason for her, or any of them, to suspect he was anything other than a member of the community. Their watchers hadn't actually been watching, just making sure they were seen.

While they'd been waiting by the creek, someone had

pressed two of the long wooden tables together, giving them room enough to all be seated without jabbing elbows.

Five and five: Henry, Zacarías, Joad, Benjamin, and himself for the town. If there'd been any way to remove himself from the table, Gabriel would have taken it, but no matter how many times he explained the idea to them, it was clear that they didn't understand, not truly. No fault on their intelligence, they simply didn't have his training. And, bluntly, he didn't trust any of them to be able to react quickly if something went wrong.

Gabriel needed to be there, to make sure that things went the way they should.

For all the seriousness of the moment, there were still moments Gabriel found himself wanting, inappropriately, to laugh. If they'd eyed and identified Gabriel as a Rider, they were clearly having difficulties with Zacarías, between his accent and his robes, the rough brown cloth covering him from shoulder to boots, the string of wooden beads wrapped around his wrist with the sigil resting in his palm.

"You're a preacherman?"

The one with the northern accent had given his name as Gauthier. He was a square-shouldered, blunt-nosed man of about Gabriel's age. Gabriel would definitely have called him out as a Rider, both for the distance he'd traveled from home and the way he kept track of his surroundings, calmly but with quiet and steady interest. A Rider, or a soldier.

"I am a son of the Holy Church," Zacarías said calmly, accepting a mug of tea from Margaret, and making room for her on the bench next to him. "But my presence here is as a member of this town, and a voice for these people."

"Just as well. God's not so much with listening in the Territory."

"I find that God listens everywhere." Zacarías' smile was small, but his eyes were calm, and for an odd moment Gabriel was reminded of Old Woman Who Never Dies. "It is if *we* listen that is the question."

"As interesting as it might be to watch you two argue theology," another of the bandits said, "this ain't what we're here for." He was younger than Gauthier, and rangier, but there was a coiled violence in him riding just under his skin. Not an angry man, Gabriel thought, nothing that simple. This was a man who held a grudge until it was cold, then ate it with relish. Gauthier named him Paul, while the others were Longfellow, a sallow-skinned man as tall as his name, a small, mean-looking woman named Kate, and the woman Gabriel had met before, Dag.

Kate looked to have Pohoug blood in her somewhere, and Gauthier was likely metís, same as Gabriel, but the others were white as salt, and all five looked to be nobody's fool.

"Do you speak for your entire camp?" Henry took lead as they'd discussed, keeping the attention on him, with Zacarías' robes as a secondary distraction. Preachermen weren't exactly rare in the Territory, but Spanish monks assuredly were, and Gabriel was counting on that to put the bandits slightly on edge, and keep their attention off *him*.

"I do," Paul agreed. "And you're the, what, headsman of this town?"

"They trust me to speak for them."

"Huh. Hope they trust you to listen for them, too, then."

Henry let his lips curl in what was almost a smile. "If you say something that is worth our hearing, yes."

"Stay calm," Gabriel had told him over breakfast that morning. "Drop a little amusement into your voice if you can, like you're listening to a child tell you about their day, listening without taking them all too seriously, but nothing that they could grab onto as giving offense."

Paul leaned forward, folding his hands together on the table. Every inch of his body proclaimed his wholehearted sincerity, and Gabriel felt the urge to reach for his knife in gut-reaction. "Then hear this, for all of them. We've been watching you. We know you're farmers and traders, craftsmen... and you're out here all alone."

There was to be no gentle wooing, then.

Henry didn't blink, but smiled back at him, a deeper, gentle smile that hid no teeth, and said, "Tua and P'wei are here as well."

"And they leave you alone, and you return the favor. Whatever agreement you made with them when you took this land, it didn't make you brothers." Paul's smile was equally toothy and leaned back slightly as though he'd just made his winning point.

"But we did make Agreement, and have upheld it," Henry replied. "And we maintain peaceful trade with them both. As you also know, from your... observations."

Gabriel stretched his leg forward slightly, under the table, and nudged Zacarías' robed leg gently, a reminder. The monk coughed into his fist, drawing everyone's attention.

"I realize that I am a stranger here, not born to the Territory as you all are, and much of this 'agreement' you speak of is still of an oddness to me. But it seems simple enough: we have been given claim to this land and the well within, and you may not take it from us. Your threats, and we recognize them as that, are nothing more than air."

"Impotent, even," Margaret said, then bit her lip as though to stifle a laugh. Gabriel could read the tension in her shoulders, but hopefully the bandits could not.

"You should not feel so confident." Longfellow spoke for the first time, his voice a painful-sounding crackle of ice. "We are a long way from the devil's stronghold, and he has greater issues to worry at than a small town in the middle of nowhere reaching an... unfortunate disappearance."

Henry's head lifted at that, and Gabriel arranged his fingers against the table in subtle tradesign for 'no.' It wasn't enough, not yet. But he could feel the potential for violence rise in the room, like the thickening of the air before a storm. His gaze flicked across the townsfolk, seeing only surprise and a hint of outrage at the overt threat, not fear or concern. If he could feel it, the ratcheting of tension in the bodies across the table, surely the others could as well?

But mayhap not. They'd been protected for so long, isolated within their town, they might not recognize it for what it was.

Gabriel braced himself, casting about for a way to redirect the conversation without tipping their hand too obviously, when Joad stepped into the silence, his natural impatience driving him.

"What do you mean by that? Not the threat, that was plain as a blight on corn. But about the devil being distracted."

Well, that was one way to do it. "He means the Americans are pushing at the eastern border," Gabriel responded, letting his fingers relax and stretching his body to take up more eye-space, drawing their attention to him. "And there are folk who should know better, thinking that the Agreement failing might not be so bad, that the world should be for them as can grab it, and no other rules apply." He let his gaze meet the eyes of every bandit across the table from him, noting the moment Dag finally pegged him for the Rider she'd met on the road.

"Paul," she said in a low voice, the single word a warning, and her leader's eyes narrowed as he suddenly took more notice of Gabriel. His skin prickled under that gaze, the thrum of something filling his ears, and he had the sudden thought that he'd missed something, something important.

Gabriel was no trained brawler, but he'd gotten into a fight or three and he knew what to look for. The way they moved, turning so that they kept the room in sight without ever losing track of the others—they'd done this before. The camp they were in –now—had it been a town once, before they came? Who had they driven from their homes, to take possession of it?

Mouse-Face's words came back to him, and he felt a shudder deep in his brain.

He shook it off. It didn't matter. *Now* mattered.

"You've been out there," Paul said, turning his full attention to Gabriel. "You know."

Gabriel inclined his head slightly, not agreeing but not disagreeing, either. Draw the other man in, force him to show his hand, then he could determine their tactics, decide the next play.

"If the devil cannot keep out the Americans, cannot keep out the Spanish," and Paul nodded his chin at Zacarías as though he were a fully-armed soldier rather than an unarmed monk, "then do you truly think he can protect you here? The tribes already wrestle each other for hunting land, do you think they will allow you to remain once the Devil's Hand is removed?"

Gabriel wondered at the man's reaction if he told him that the Devil's Hand was not only not removed, but a few days' ride from him. He contemplated saying just that, then, regretfully, let it go.

"The Tui would not harm the town. They have given the tribe no offense."

"You think that will matter, when the Agreement fails? You think they don't want that well, too? That land you've got growing? Think they won't just come down and take it, soon's they can? Better to let us in, let us protect you before it does happen."

Margaret shifted, looking uncomfortable, and Joad's jaw clenched, his skin going pale under the pressure. Gabriel hoped that they were playing along, but he had a moment's fear that the bandit's words were getting through, pushing them where they hadn't known they were raw.

"And then what?" Henry asked, his voice tight. "You will kill the tribes before they can attack us? Take their hunting lands? And after that, what? When will you be satisfied?"

"He doesn't want the land," Gabriel said suddenly, feeling the odd pieces clattering into place, the tension on his skin suddenly too familiar. "He doesn't even want the well itself. He wants the water. *All* the water."

Paul grinned, and if the teeth hadn't been human-flat, Gabriel would have reached for salt, assuming it was a ghoul or demon across the table from him, so flat and cold were his eyes. He almost did reach for salt anyway, before remembering that the stick was tucked into his saddle bags, in the shed with Steady and well out of reach.

Old Woman Who Never Dies' tribe would have been within their rights to leave Gabriel on the banks, feverish and near death. Graciendo would have been within rights to kill him when he stumbled, half-mad, into his winter den.

They hadn't, for one simple reason: The Agreement wasn't about debt, or obligation. It was about *intent*.

The people of Rabbit's Mound had brought him here under misleading hospitality, had tried to bind him... but they had offered him no direct harm. Had intended no-one harm to him, or –anyone—anything—else. What this man wanted.

Paul Gauthier would turn them into slaves.

"Water's gonna be the new silver," the bandit said, unashamed. "And a well like you've got there, deep and sweet and protected seven ways from Saturday? Magic'd so it never runs dry? When the time comes, that'll make us kings in this land.

"And it's not like we're gonna kick you out or anything." His voice softened, reasonable as a preacher at a baby-naming. "You keep on as you were, growing and weaving and doing what you do. We'll take care of the rest."

The worst thing was, Gabriel knew, *knew* that it wasn't a

bad-faith offer. It wasn't a good -faith one, either, but on the surface it wasn't bad. And it had the underlying value of truth: eventually, the Agreement would fail. The devil knew it, even as he sent Isobel cross-Territory, fixing what she could.

All Henry and the others had to do was accept the bandits' offer and they could stop worrying, stop trying to find protection, because they'd have it.

Against everything except their protectors.

"There's just one problem with that," he heard himself saying as though from a long distance away. "What if the water doesn't want *you?*"

10

The moment the word left his mouth, Gabriel wanted to kick himself. This wasn't what he'd planned, at all. He'd hoped to push the bandits into making a mistake, into doing something that would draw the weight of the Agreement down on them. Logic. Persuasion. Those were the tools he'd been trained to use.

But their leader was too smart, too calm; Gabriel suspected that he was using the same plan on them, or one similar enough, and with the utter arrogance of the man's 'offer,' the odds on who would break first were not in the town's favor.

So. A pivot.

Gabriel wasn't Isobel, to command any kind of obedience just by his presence. He wasn't even a marshal, or a Judge, that he could state the Law and have it stick. He'd been an Advocate, but in a place far from here, where all the rules were different. All the rules save one: don't lose.

If your opponent is holding all the cards, bring in a new deck.

He grinned, the cockiest, most self-assured grin he'd ever built, and asked again, "What if the water doesn't want you?"

"Are you mad?" The look of tolerant amusement on the bandit's face made Gabriel's teeth clench behind the grin, rage not entirely his own tightening his muscles and making his stomach sick.

He could feel the spirit-snake slithering along his arm, smell the stink of Graciendo's fur, hear the flickerthwack of the devil's cards. He heard the words of the river-witch, back down in Red Stick. *"Everything's got a price; what matters is how you pay it. Everything's an agreement. Else it's something else, less pretty, less kind, and far less binding."*

Henry was right: the folk of this town were not soldiers, were barely even hunters. And he, Gabriel, had been right: one man alone could not stop them. But this... he could feel something other than himself surging in his veins, wet and fierce and unstoppable.

His choice, what he would do with it.

Gabriel pushed down the rage and lifted his chin, shaping his words as though he were back before the Bench, arguing for a man's –life—or death. "You come into our home and you speak as though it were simply a matter of... Of violence. Or the threat of violence. As though water or bone or wind can be claimed. As though we are the ones making the decisions."

They were all staring at him now, but he thought the woman, Dag, had a flicker of understanding, and Zacarías...if anyone else here understood what the Territory was, it would be the monk, if he'd allowed himself to truly remember even half of what had happened up on that hill, when the Hand and a magician had saved their sorry selves from magic the Territory had reshaped into something new...

"We're all here on sufferance," Gabriel went on, his gaze passing over them all, one by one. "Not the tribes, not the devil's. They're just trying to teach us the rules." Or, in Isobel's case, enforce them. Not for the sakes of those who broke them, but for everyone else. To keep the Territory safe for the rest.

"Saying you'll claim the water, control it? That's like... like a magician saying he'll claim the wind. You've got to pay for it. You've got to pay what *they* ask. And you've got to have permission. Otherwise it'll turn on you."

Magicians petitioned the winds and went mad when they took on that magic. Mad, and not—quite—human. Claiming water...

Water-child. The sensation of drowning, the dry-fever that wracked him when he tried to leave, swelled his throat with a too-familiar panic, and his fingers clenched at the wooden table in front of him.

"What, you think the water will object to who draws it?" The sallow-skinned bandit scoffed, glancing sideways at his companions as though inviting them to share his amusement.

"I think," Gabriel said softly, "that if you try to force the issue, you will regret it."

Wind was magic and bone was magic, but water... water was life.

They knew the town had no real defense. But the well did.

The first settlers had invited the Tua to perform a medicine dance when it was dug. Medicine like that would settle into the well, wrap around it. Change it. Empower it.

Gabriel could feel the surge of that power within him. But was it simply the well, or something more?

It was a risk he wasn't sure he could take.

"This is nonsense," the other woman said, and he heard the scratch and thud of chairs being pushed back, the scrape of metal on leather.

"It's been illuminating, speaking with you," Paul said, standing in a more leisurely fashion, his hand clear of his knives, but Gabriel did not make the mistake of thinking he was harmless, and neither did those around him. Just because you could not win a fight did not mean you should not fight it.

His fingers closed around the hilt of his larger blade, sliding it free from the sheath and flipping it up into ready pose, even as he saw Zacarías reaching for something under the –table—a stick the width of a thumb, and the length of his arm. The monk slid it through both hands, squaring his feet. Joad had his knife out, a heavy, curved thing that could likely chop through deer bone without hesitation.

He felt his body move, the chair sliding back as he got to his feet and had the odd sensation of watching as though through someone else's eyes, distanced from where he was.

He did not have to do this. He could let go, not-answer. What did it matter to him what this town decided, so long as they survived?

It mattered.

It seemed impossibly simple now. Gabriel felt the fear, the frustration and the anger, layers of it built like scabs over resentment, but none of that changed the Touch laid on him at birth. Water claimed him. The Territory claimed him. He'd been running from it his entire life, terrified of drowning. And yet...

He'd been terrified by what he saw in Red Stick, the creeping sickness infecting people, turning them mean and foolish, ready to turn on each other for gain and for fear. Terrified, and furious, and all the more so for watching Isobel sink deeper and deeper into what she was, letting the Territory's medicine, the devil's machinations, reshape her into something he could not understand.

Mentoring was about teaching them how to survive. But he didn't know how to help her survive that. So, he'd gone to rage at the River, expecting that it would take him, drown him... maybe, in his darkest thoughts, turn him into a thing that *could* help Isobel. Or simply to end him.

Instead... it had let him go.

The blurred fog cleared, and he could see, now. It had claimed him. But he had not claimed it.

Intent mattered.

Gabriel pressed the soles of his boots into the floor, lifted his spine the way he would settling into Steady' saddle, pushed himself deep into the ground like roots, spreading and searching until he tapped at the bright trickle of water deep below. But it moved too slow, too thinly, and he extended his Touch further, feeling for the water that fed the well itself, deeper below.

Hello?

Nothing. He felt a moment's disappointment mixed with relief, and the latter made him angry enough to try again.

"The moment someone moves, they will have given offense." Henry, still trying to follow Gabriel's script, as best he could, while Margaret moved to his left shoulder, another staff in her hands. They must have arranged to have them stashed underneath, when the tables were being moved together. Gabriel had a moment to thank fortune for foresight, before something tugged at him, pulling his attention down and inward again.

Cool crisp bright gave way to *dark still deep* and a sense of *curiosity* pushing back at him. Gabriel shuddered, instinctively wanting nothing more than to pull away from the touch.

Instead, he ripped off the scabs, even those still new-formed and blooded, and let the River in.

He stood in a river, red clay cliffs rising on other side, the sky storm-grey overhead. Water swirled around his ankles, then his knees, clear one moment then muddy the next, the faint swipe of things moving below the surface, brushing against his legs. He blinked, and the water was rising to his hips, lapping at his fingertips.

If he let it rise further, if it submerged him, he would drown. And yet, Gabriel felt no fear, no panic.

He had said no to the Mudwater and... it had let him go. Now he returned, not to offer himself as sacrifice, or demand answers, but to ask for help. One part of the greater whole to another.

He exhaled, and let the waters rise over his head, filling his lungs and washing away his thoughts, taking every worry, every fear, every shred of anger and love. He was empty, sodden, nameless, lost.

And then it washed it all back into him, ice-cold and sharp-clear, and he surfaced again.

"Stop." Gabriel lifted his head, feeling moisture coat his skin like he was back south again, the air filled with wet, and said it again, louder. "Stop."

Nobody'd drawn blood yet, nobody'd used their weapon; how much time had passed while he was submerged in the water-sense? Gabriel shook the question aside, the thoughts in his head sloshing unpleasantly. "You need to stop. Step back."

"And who's going to make us, Rider? You?"

Not him. "I'm..." The words fought to stay behind his teeth; he pushed them out, the river below him surging up through his veins. "I'm water-child and I tell you, the water doesn't want you." Want was not the right word, but he did not have the right word, not in all the languages he knew. "If you try..." He coughed, his throat too soaked to swallow properly. "If you interfere with the folk who were given the blessing, it will rise in response, and wash us from the land."

Water wore things down slowly, wave after wave, but it could also surge over its banks, and when it did it could not distinguish between one pebble and the next. It could not tell resident from bandit, crops from weed. It would drown everything.

"Water child, huh? Tell the water *this*," Longfellow said, and lunged, the bone-handled knife in his hand cutting under Gabriel's jacket and stabbing under his ribs.

He felt the knife go in, sliding into the flesh, but the expected pain didn't come. He glanced down as though to confirm that the knife had made contact and saw the bone handle sticking out, blood already staining the metal. He could hear shouting, yelling, and felt hands on his back, the scuffle of feet and chairs around him, but couldn't react, staring dumbly at the blade. He'd been cut before, knives and claws, and they had all hurt like the seven blazes. Why not this?

He touched the handle, and water dripped from his fingers onto the blade, washing the blood away. He stared at the drops, too bright and clear to be sweat, and lifted two fingers to his lips, tongue licking the moisture away. It was musty, musky with salt and sulfur, and a shudder ran down his spine that had nothing to do his injury.

"So be it," a voice said from his mouth, and he *felt* the creek rise, spilling over its –banks—not just here, but in the bandit's camp as well, the water following his lead, silt and salt filling wells and cisterns. A sense of horror filled him, matched only by a darker satisfaction.

"Gabriel. Gabriel, imbécil!" There was a howl and a thump, the sound of wood hitting flesh, and a shocked, echoing silence. "Stay *down,*" the monk said to someone else, his voice a rumble of thunder, and Gabriel swayed, thinking that must be the sound of his god, roaring down at the sinners.

"Let it go!" and the monk was speaking to him now, Gabriel thought. He let his hand drop from the blade and looked up. The bandits were down, two face down on the ground, the others on their knees, two people he did not know holding ancient-looking blunderbusses in the ready, while Joad clenched his deer-sticker in both hands, his body singing with the need to use it on someone.

The monk was speaking Spanish now, so quickly Gabriel could barely understand him. "Let it go, Gabriel. Whatever it is that you do, whatever it does through you, stop it!"

Oh. But he hadn't done anything, he wanted to protest. He'd just bled, and...

Salt and sulphur. The feel of Old Bear's claw on his lip. The warm feel of drowning...

Water-child, the river-witch had called him. But children grow and become themselves.

Oh.

He staggered into Zacarías' arms, drained and dropping, folding himself back into flesh again. Water surged in his veins, then subsided back into blood.

The monk touched under Gabriel's shirt, and whatever he saw there made him blaspheme under his breath. "Fetch Joseph!"

11

His wound had been bleed freely under the chirurgeon's close attention until he was satisfied that no rot had set in, then he'd been tucked onto a cot in a small room off the main hall, since he could not climb the loft he'd been given. Three full days after that were spent sleeping restlessly, someone feeding him broth until he could feel it pressing from within and the need to pee drove him to his feet, staggering across the room to use the pot, then staggering back to bed, until he felt the need to do it again.

Beyond him, Gabriel had the sense of waters surging, currents of salt and sulfur running through the clear crispness of stone-fresh streams, and the squelch of mud under the feet of people passing by. He knew without asking that the waters had drawn back, and hoped that the winter crops hadn't been ruined, that no homes had been flooded, before he dropped back off to sleep.

At one point, he opened his eyes to see Henry standing at his side, hat in his hand, and a look of constipated regret on his face.

"I'm not sorry. For bringing you here. For... keeping you here. But I am sorry you were hurt."

Gabriel would have laughed, if it didn't hurt so much. "That's mighty generous of you."

"You were supposed to apologize." Greta came up behind him, glaring fiercely at her husband.

"I just did!"

"That was a sad excuse for an apology, and you should be ashamed of yourself." She scowled at him again for good measure, then reached down to pat Gabriel's shoulder, like a sparrow attempting to console an ox. "Joseph says you can sit up and eat a proper meal now, if you're ready for it. I've brought fresh bread, and some bits of chicken."

He allowed as how he might be able to do that, now.

Greta fussed about, settling a tray across Gabriel's lap and tucking blankets behind him in case he tired while sitting up, while Henry pulled the sole chair in the room closer to the cot, and sat down.

"You did all that? Call the waters up?"

"Not me." A half-truth. "What happened? Don't look at me like that; I truly don't know." Or, he knew only what the waters had shown him, and was blessedly forgetting most of it, already.

"Creek rose, came over the banks like a flash storm had hit, even though there wasn't a cloud in the sky. Ran up every path like it was heading for home, straight uphill. Never seen water do that before, never want to see it again. And the well..."

Henry's eyes were haunted by more than the grey shadow under his lids.

"Glad I missed all that." He didn't bother asking if the wellwater was drinkable again; it would be, eventually.

"You should be more glad we decided to keep your part in all that quiet," the old man said, clearly ignoring Gabriel's denial of responsibility. "Blamed the bandits, claimed it was the well's medicine coming after 'em."

"And people believed it." Of course they did, people would believe anything, especially if it made them feel safer. And it was not entirely an untruth.

"Helps that the Tua elders are coming down, rise of the new moon, to do their thing over the well, clean it out and appease it or whatever it is they do." Henry didn't seem to be a man of religion, white or native, but his tone was that of a man who would refuse no aid.

Much like the town's founder. Wise men, both of them.

"And the bandits?" He remembered at least one going down, but after that it was a foggy blank.

"Hauled 'em to the bridge and booted 'em over. Told 'em if we saw them again, even at a distance, we'd shoot instead of talking nice."

Gabriel had his doubt that the guns he'd seen in use here were accurate enough to kill a man, as old as they were, but he suspected they'd not lack volunteers to try.

"You might want to change the town's name," he said, settling back into the pillow with a sigh. "Rabbit's Swim, maybe?"

"You best stick to Riding and not naming," Henry said gruffly. "We just want to put this behind us, not linger in it."

Gabriel didn't doubt that. He also suspected they weren't going to have much choice in the matter once word got around, and it assuredly would. But that would be their problem, not his.

IT WAS another two days before Gabriel was able to leave the cot without feeling as though he'd been stabbed, but the sticky, tacky feeling of salt water lingered on his skin no matter how many passes he made with a damp cloth, how often he dried himself off. Eventually, he resigned himself to living with it, grateful it was only a trace.

Henry was a regular visitor during those days, with Gerta and Joseph the chirurgeon close second, but other than that, he saw no-one, only hearing their voices outside. Henry might have blamed the bandits, but the coincidence of him coming to town just before all this all happened, Gabriel knew it would be too much for most.

"You rode off without the mule? Or supplies?"

The irony of a Greenie monk lecturing him was not lost on –Gabriel—nor Gerta or Henry, from the sly grins they – exchanged—but he supposed he had earned it.

"I was able to trade for basics at the mercantile," he said, frowning at Gerta as she took a shirt out of his pack and shook it out, then tossed it onto the pile she'd said was for washing. "About a week's ride southeast?" He thought it was that long, but wasn't quite certain

Henry was looking at him oddly, his earlier smile nowhere in sight now. "There's no mercantile for a week's ride or more. There's nothing at all the way you came, save a few winter camps, until you come to Blackback Creek."

"There is," Gabriel said, frowning back at him. "I bought the coalstone you're holding, there."

Henry put the coalstone back down on Gabriel's pack with more haste than was seemly for a grown man. "This mercantile. You catch the shopkeep's name?"

"Nashon. Odd fellow with an odder partner?"

The three of them looked at each other, Greta's eyes wide, Zacarías' worried.

Gabriel thought of the spirit-snake, of Graciendo lingering at his campfire, and the tree that grew out of nothing, and made note to tell none of that to them, if this was how they reacted to a relatively ordinary transaction. "Come now, Mouse-Face was a surprise, I'll grant, but—"

"There is no mercantile there," Henry said again. "There was a settlement, once. Long ago. Odd folk, scholars, only men. Led by a man named Nashon. They set up a camp in land nobody'd claim, and for good reason. And then they... disappeared."

Gabriel's eyebrows raised. "Disappeared?"

"Men, horses, buildings. Lost in a mountain mist, and when the mist cleared, they were gone. Most assumed they'd annoyed a spirit. But that was nearly fifty years past. There's been nothing built there, since then."

The expressions on their faces... Gabriel had seen it with Isobel, too many times, even with those who didn't know what she was. Even those who should have known better, who'd been born to the winds and waters of the Territory, too often thought the world was as they saw it, with nothing hidden below or above. He tried to imagine a spirit-snake visiting any of them and had to bite back a burst of inappropriate laughter.

"They seemed remarkably solid for haints," he said, "and content in each other, whatever had befallen them." Mouse-Face had spoken of others, as well. So they were not alone. "And a wise man never refuses aid." He took the pack back from Henry, tucking the coalstone away and out of sight.

"Even for the Territory, you have stories," Zacarías said finally, when the others seemed struck dumb by his nonchalance. "I will pray for the health of your soul."

Gabriel ran a hand through his hair, feeling how long the strands were getting, thinking he might ask Gerta to cut it before he left, and said nothing in response.

THE VISITS TAPERED off after that, to Gabriel's lack of surprise, and when a day later Joseph deemed him well enough to move, he wasted no further time. Gathering his belongings back into the pack, he –went—slowly—to reclaim his horse, thankful that the walk from hall to shed was short enough that he did not encounter anyone.

It might be rude to leave without farewells, but he had not yet forgotten or forgiven Henry's earlier trick, and with the tribal elders coming for the ceremony, Gabriel wanted to be gone by then. A man's business might be his own, but a Water Society member would have no hesitation about asking questions of him he still wasn't sure he could answer.

He might have been imagining things, but he thought Steady was glad to see him, the gelding reaching over to huff at his hair and nip on his sleeve when he came close. "I see you stayed nice and dry." The old rugs underfoot had doubtless seen worse than rising water in their time, but they were dry and dusty with straw, with no hint of mold or damp. "You were bored, were you? Only so much rest and grooming you could manage?"

After checking to make sure that the horse had in fact been well-cared for while he was abed, Gabriel bent, carefully, to pick up the saddle, wincing a little as he lifted it.

"Stand still and let's do this easy, all right?" he said, and Steady's left ear twitched once, his flanks shuddering as the weighted leather came down on his back, and the belly-band wrapped around.

"No tricks this time? You must be as eager to be going as I am," he told the gelding, sliding the bit into his mouth and waiting until the beast had mouthed it into place.

There was a creak of the door sliding open behind them, and Gabriel tensed for a moment.

"So. You're riding on."

Zacarías. Gabriel finished adjusting the bridle and slapped the gelding affectionately on the neck. "Your hospitality's been... interesting, but yeah, I'm riding on."

"If you must, then."

He came around to face the monk, raising an eyebrow at the canvas bag hanging by a strap from the monk's hand.

"This..." Zacarías lifted it, offering it to him. "Some supplies, for your journey. It was the least we could do, after..."

After chaining him to the town, after forcing him to do things none of them wanted to acknowledge? Gabriel didn't say any of that, but merely took the bag, his nose identifying yeast and sour curds.

"It won't keep for long, but..." The Spaniard's voice kept trailing off, as though he were swallowing words.

"It's appreciated." Fresh bread and cheese were things the Road didn't supply much of; he'd enjoy them until they were gone. "Not sure where I'm heading next, but I doubt I'll see fresh-made bread any time soon."

"You could stay," the monk blurted out. "If you were not heading anywhere in particular." Zacarías looked at the horse then, then at the roof, anywhere but directly at Gabriel. "The town... I know you only stayed because Henry bound you, but it's a good place to be, and will be better without the threat of bandits hanging overhead. If you had nowhere else calling you."

Gabriel turned away, latching the canvas bag to the rest of his packs, taking a moment longer than necessary to make sure it was secure. "I'm not a farmer, or a weaver, or anything that's needed here."

"It's not about what the town needs. It's about what you need. What your soul needs."

Gabriel chuckled then, reaching out to slap a hand against the other man's shoulder. "And there's the monk I've been expecting. I'm a Rider, Zac. I'm best on the Road."

Zacarías ignored the nickname. "A Rider, riding to what? If it is true, that the Agreement is failing, if all that we are building is for naught, then what good does running ahead of it do?"

"It keeps you one step ahead." Everything set and latched, he adjusted his hat securely, and pulled the gloves from his jacket pocket, taking Steady's reins up in the other hand to lead him out. "Take care of yourself, Brother Zacarías."

"I will pray for you, Gabriel."

"You do that."

SIMPLY BEING in the saddle again made the lingering pain in his torso and chest fade, the familiar stretch-and-press of riding more comfortable to him than walking, and the reassuring rock of the gelding's four legs underneath him soothing as a lullaby. It took far less time than he'd anticipated to reach the road where Henry had hailed him a little over a week before. He'd thought they'd traveled further, that night in the rain.

Perhaps they had.

Gabriel reined Steady in, looking out and ahead, toward the north.

He'd had a reason to be heading that way, he was reasonable sure of it. But at just that moment the reason seemed far distant, as far as the hazy blue blur of the mountains on the horizon.

The Agreement was failing. He'd known that, even before the bandit had spoken. He'd seen it, with every incident Isobel responded to, every argument made about why this should be allowed, or that. The looks of the people in Red Stick, the skittishness of the native folk they encountered, the fears the chiefs couldn't bring themselves to name. The way the marshals were spread thin now, with so many people settling in and setting roots, bringing their kin and spawn and problems.

"A Rider, riding to what?" Zacarías had asked.

Gabriel thought of the tree, growing overnight from nothing save restless dreams and despair. Stone for bones, roots for veins; the marshal's sigil, enclosed by the glow of the rising sun. *Justice, justice thou shalt pursue.*

Gabriel was not a marshal. But he thought of the waters rising, still whispering in his veins. He felt the Road beneath him, and remembered what he had taught Isobel, that anyone could reach the Road, if they listened.

The devil had known. Had he seen the future, when he stood on the banks and told the would-be conquistadors that they could not have this land? Had all this been to buy them time—time for children to be born into the Territory, to have the Touch on them, to bind them to it so they might not leave? To ensure that against every new settler, there was someone who *belonged*?

If so, from a logical, tactical view, it was brilliant, the brilliance born of desperation, under the weight of inevitability. And Gabriel had played his part, however unwilling. He'd given way to the illness that brought him back within the Territory's borders. He had mentored the Hand, giving them another layer of protection, pushing the inevitable out a little further—a month? A year? A decade? How much would have been enough?

He should be angry– he should be furious. He'd been used, played the way the devil shuffled his card, exactly as he'd sworn he never would be.

Graciendo's warnings echoed in his head and his own uncertainties hung low and heavy in his heart. But where fury should have been, he found... resignation. Amusement. The memory of Isobel's sigh, and the flickerthwack noise of the devil's cards against green felt, and the gentle push of water running against his legs.

You've healed, Graciendo had said.

Mayhap. Mayhap not.

He'd dreamed of being someone else, once. But this, his horse under him and the Road ahead; this was good, too. The banter of Nashon and Mouse-Face, caught out of time. The grumbling of Graciendo, even the sly insinuation of the spirit-snake. The unnamed village building itself under the unsleeping rage of the firebird's haint, and Rabbit's Mound and Andreas, and even Red Stick, as roiled as it was right now.

"The river runs, the mountains rise and fall, the winds shatter, and the bones... the bones remain. Remember that," the devil had told him. *"The bones remain."*

Maybe there would be enough time. The Dust Roads were built from their bones, after all. Build enough roads, and everything stayed connected.

Picking up the reins again, Gabriel pressed his heels in, and they rode on.

AUTHOR'S NOTE

So yeah, GABRIEL'S ROAD is in your hands a few months later than I'd originally planned. That's on me. A lot of us are writing more slowly than we used to — living in America in the 20teens is exhausting — but I had this sucker all plotted and planned out, so it should have been an easy 6 months in and out.

Yeah. Not so much.

A year ago, I didn't know this story would be so difficult to write. The first draft went fast, but it was.... not right. Probably because, although I knew what happened, I didn't actually know what the story was *about*.

Lemme 'splain.

From the very beginning of SILVER ON THE ROAD, I knew that Gabriel didn't have his shit together, although he had a very pretty façade going. While Isobel was facing a traditional coming-of-age, he was coming up to his Second Chance, the opportunity to stop running and finally put down some roots like a grown-ass adult. And for most of the story, that's how we played it. Until about halfway through RED WATERS RISING, when I realized that he'd been hiding much worse damage than even I knew.

And you can't put down roots with that much damage — the first storm that comes along will just uproot you again.

And as I drew Gabriel along this part of his journey, a lot of small, unexpected details both in his actions and his reactions started to feel very familiar to me.

Sometimes the writer lizard-brain hides things from you, to make sure that you don't trip over your own emotional feet. So there was a lot of sitting back in my chair and going "huh," happening for a few months, until my front mammal brain caught up with what my lizard brain had been doing.

Sneaky, story-smart, lizard brain.

I've written about my own PTSD*. I've written characters experiencing PTSD before (FREE FALL, "Apparent Horizon," and a few others). But I had never written a character going through therapy for it before. But that's exactly what Gabriel undergoes in this story. and as I look back now, I realize I've been writing my own Journey as well.

Neither Gabriel nor I am 'cured' or 'fixed' or 'done.' We never will be. But we'll be okay.

(By the way, Graciendo is a *terrible* therapist. 10/10 would not recommend.)

— Laura Anne

*as part of the #holdontothelight mental health essay series, which I highly recommend to anyone wondering 'is it just me?'

ACKNOWLEDGMENTS

As ever, I owe a huge note of thanks to the members of the WordWarRoom, who were there at all odd hours of the day (and night). Also to Mindi Welton-Mitchell, who didn't realize she was helping me work out plot-issues when we discussed theology...
And all the readers who have been patient, and only sent a *few* sad-kitten-eyed email wondering when this book would be out.

ALSO BY LAURA ANNE GILMAN

The Devil's West

Silver on the Road

The Cold Eye

Red Waters Rising

West Winds' Fool and Other Stories of the Devil's West

Other works available via Book View Cafe

From Whence You Came: A Lands Vin Novella

Darkly Human: 18 Stories

Dragon Virus

Sylvan Investigations

Miles to Go

Promises to Keep

The Work of Hunters

An Interrupted Cry

ABOUT THE AUTHOR

Laura Anne Gilman's work has been hailed as "a true American myth" by NPR, and praised for her "deft plotting and first-class characters" by Publishers Weekly. She has won the Endeavor Award for THE COLD EYE, and been shortlisted for a Nebula, (another) Endeavor, and a Washington State Book Award. Her novels include the Locus-bestselling weird western Devil's West trilogy, the Cosa Nostradamus urban fantasy series, and the Vineart War trilogy, and the story collections WEST WINDS' FOOL and DARKLY HUMAN.

A former New Yorker, she currently lives outside of Seattle with two cats and many deadlines. More information, social media links, and updates can be found at www.lauraannegilman.net.

ABOUT BOOK VIEW CAFÉ

Book View Café Publishing Cooperative (BVC) is an author-owned cooperative of over fifty professional writers, publishing in a variety of genres such as fantasy, romance, mystery, and science fiction.

BVC authors include New York Times and USA Today bestsellers; Nebula, Hugo, and Philip K. Dick Award winners; World Fantasy Award, Campbell Award, and RITA Award nominees; and winners and nominees of many other publishing awards.

Since its debut in 2008, BVC has gained a reputation for producing high-quality ebooks, and is now bringing that same quality to its print editions.

www.bookviewcafe.com